The War Nickel Murders

The War Nickel Murders

D.P. Benjamin

ELEVATION PRESS
OF COLORADO

The War Nickel Murders
by D.P. Benjamin

Copyright © 2024 by Donald Paul Benjamin

For more information, please see *About the Author* at the close of this book and visit benjaminauthor.com

Cover photo by D.P. Benjamin.
Cover design and interior design and formatting by Donna Marie Benjamin.

All characters and events in this novel, other than those clearly in the public domain, are fictitious and any resemblance to real persons, living or dead, is purely coincidental.

All rights reserved. No part of this publication may be reproduced, distributed, or transmitted in any form or by any means, including photocopying, recording, or other electronic or mechanical methods, without the prior written permission of the publisher, except in the case of brief quotations embodied in critical reviews and certain other noncommercial uses permitted by copyright law. For permission requests, write to the publisher, addressed "Attention: Permission Coordinator," at the address below:

Elevation Press of Colorado
P.O. Box 603
Cedaredge, CO 81413

Ordering information: Quantity sales. Special discounts are available on quantity purchases by book clubs, corporations, associations, and others. For details, contact the publisher at the address above.

ISBN 978-0-932624-26-0

1. Main category— [Mystery-Cozy] 2. Other categories— [Colorado]—[Detective]

Cedaredge, Colorado
www.elevation-press-books.com

For information on services offered by Elevation Press of Colorado, please see the final page of this book.

For my infant sister, Ann Benjamin

So long as men can breathe or eyes can see,
So long lives this, and this gives life to thee.

Excerpt from
Sonnet 18: Shall I compare thee to a summer's day?
—William Shakespeare

Prologue

December 30, 2019 / Dawn

The bullet struck Herbert Schulz squarely in the back.

The old man pitched forward and landed hard. Dislodged by the fall, his wool cap tumbled off and was left behind. Still alive but immobilized, he slid face-down across the ice. His helpless legs and trailing ice skates drifted in his wake, and his outstretched arms seemed to be seeking something just beyond his grasp. Propelled by momentum, he traced a bloody trail upon the frozen surface of Island Lake.

Herbert's undignified slide caused his prone body to twirl completely around so that—when he came to a stop—he was facing the opposite shore. With effort, the doomed man raised his head. His wire-rimmed eyeglasses clung precariously to his face, the fragile frame twisted, and one eyepiece shattered. Staring through his ruined glasses, he could just make out the shape of a man walking toward him across the ice. He could see the rifle too and he wondered, somewhat clinically, whether the assassin would let him bleed-out or waste a second bullet.

If our roles were reversed, the dying man thought, *I'd get a little closer and take another shot—a second shot—just to make certain.*

Which is precisely what the killer did.

Chapter 1

A Fishing Trip Spoilt
(December 30, 2019 / 1:30 p.m.)

Delta County Sheriff Jack Treadway was alone on the frozen expanse of Crawford Reservoir. The sun was shining, tempering the chill of the frigid afternoon. He balanced on a campstool as he gripped a short-jigging rod in anticipation of spending hours appreciating the finer points of ice fishing heaven. The fish weren't biting but it was all about being outside on a glorious December day, and he deserved a break.

It had been a challenging week. The sheriff had outlasted a spate of chaotic traffic problems spawned by drifting snow and icy roads. He and his deputies had endured the challenges of rescuing stranded horses and corralling marauding cattle. They'd dealt with four deer-versus-auto collisions, three dozen fender-bender accidents, and not one, but two exploding methamphetamine laboratories. Somehow the overburdened public servant had survived in order to reach the holiday break. And he was enjoying a lazy Monday, miles away from civilization, in an isolated niche of Western Colorado.

Which is when the call came in.

"Two calling one," Lieutenant Madge Oxford's voice was unmistakable on his earpiece and her tone was urgent. "Two calling one," the efficient officer repeated.

"Treadway," he growled into his lapel microphone.

"Got a homicide, Boss," Oxford announced.

"Where?"

"Island Lake."

"I.D.?"

There was a lengthy pause before Oxford said, "Herb Schulz."

"Oh man," said Jack. "On my way. Set it up."

"Already on it, Boss," she assured the sheriff.

"Okay. Out."

Set it up, Jack told himself. *Easier said than done.*

It was late December, a period of doldrums between Christmas and New Year's, and the whole county was on break. So, setting up a homicide crime scene would mean pulling in a lot of people who had other ideas about how to spend their time off. There'd only been five homicides on Colorado's Western Slope all year, and only one in Delta County and, before that, no other county fatalities at all, going back to 2010. But apparently the county's customary trickle of violent crime had decided to end the present year by overflowing the banks.

Clearly, he told himself, *somebody didn't get the memo statin' that everybody, includin' me, has the day off.*

"What are the friggin' chances?" Sheriff Jack Treadway asked aloud. Then he frowned, knowing full-well there was no one around for miles to hear, let alone answer, his irritated question.

With a heavy sigh, the dedicated sheriff reeled in his lines, folded up his campstool, and re-packed his sled. Standing there with the sled's icy tether in his gloved hand, Jack paused for a moment to stare longingly at the perfectly round hole which he was being forced to abandon. It'd taken him twenty minutes to drill that masterpiece through the thick ice and round it off while scooping out the shavings. He hated to leave that flawless hole and invest a half-hour pulling the sled over the ice and up the snowy hillside to reach his distant vehicle. But there wasn't any choice. He was miles from the crime scene and the day was advancing.

"Back to work," Jack muttered as he started across the frozen lake with the hastily-loaded sled trailing obediently behind.

Reaching the parking lot, the sheriff stowed his gear— stubby sled and all—in the patrol car's roomy trunk. Then he fired up the dependable Dodge Charger and steered toward the roadway. To reach the faraway incident scene, he'd have to drive fifty-three miles across snowbound topography, on mostly two-lane roads, running the lights but not the siren, and working the radio as he went.

A few quick radio contacts with the Feds, the Colorado Bureau of Investigation, and the highway department confirmed that Madge was way ahead of him. So, he signed off and concentrated on the road. Cars and trucks pulled over to let him pass. A few motorists waved, although he didn't wave back.

Hands on the wheel, he told himself. That was the extent of the country-western lyrics the irritated sheriff could recall. So, he gave up, roughly hummed the rest, and drove on until it struck him that—other than a brief expression of surprise—he hadn't taken a single moment to reflect on the dead man.

The victim was a quasi-hermit who lived high up on the lofty slopes of Grand Mesa but still found time to mingle in the village. The sheriff tried to picture the old man—white hair, scruffy beard, fit for his age, a passion for wearing goofy caps, and what else? An even disposition—a World War II survivor who kept to himself but was nevertheless liked by most. Jack didn't know Herbert Schulz well, but the old man was the friend of a friend.

Leaving Highway 92 and passing through Austin, Jack bumped over the coal train tracks and chastised himself for being so upset about losing his fishing hole when Herbert Schulz had lost his life.

"Makes you think," the sheriff said aloud as he waved at a local resident walking his dog. Both master and animal were wearing matching sweaters, which made Jack smile. "Good to be alive," he decided.

The narrow pavement was damp but clear of snow and Jack made good time. He slowed down as he rolled abreast of Upper Valley Holsteins and stopped briefly to speak to a pair of sizable dogs who were guarding the household of dairy owners Andy and Polly Jo Wick.

"Max," he addressed the bigger animal. "And Lucky," he nodded to the smaller dog. "Good work, you two. So, carry on. And be sure to tell your master I appreciate your role as faithful sentinels. Glad you're on the job to mark the shoulder and keep traffic on the road and out of the ditch."

Moments later, the sheriff reached Highway 65 and turned north. Passing through the Eckert settlement, he glanced sideways wishing he could turn, cross the bridge, and follow the winding road to Lavender. Over there in the village most everyone would be at the farm, celebrating Annie Sands' December birthday. He'd been invited but had made the hard choice to miss the festivities in favor of going fishing. Now he longed, more than ever, to have the leisure to recant that decision.

It was a fleeting thought and the hopeful idea of spending time with the living would have to wait. Like it or not, the sheriff was obliged to keep his appointment with death.

Fifteen minutes later, he reached Cedaredge where he stopped for coffee and fuel. Standing at the small town's roadside mini-mart, Jack looked up from the gas pump and studied the clouds building up over Grand Mesa. The 11,000-foot flat-topped mountain stretched from east to west, a broad expanse which dominated the northern skyline. The clouds above it looked dark and ominous.

"Might snow," said the driver in the next bay.

"Might," said Jack as he nodded to his neighbor.

Guiding his patrol car back onto Highway 65, the sheriff neared Main Street and punched the siren as he ran the town's one stoplight. Leaving the snowbound orchards of the Surface Creek Valley behind, he kept the roof lights flashing and started uphill.

It was spitting snow and Jack took the curves too fast, but the road was clear of ice as he zigzagged seventeen miles up the southern flanks of Grand Mesa. His destination was the staging area his crew had established on a bluff overlooking Island Lake. It was mid-afternoon and, despite his empathy for the dead man, the sheriff had to admit he was still smarting from the disappointment of having to interrupt his long-postponed ice fishing trip, not to mention missing Annie's party. As if designed to interrupt his unproductive daydreaming, a snowplow passed, motoring downhill with its blade up. The driver tooted his strident horn as the behemoth truck passed Jack's ascending patrol car and both men exchanged a wave.

Clouds blocked the sun, but it had stopped snowing when at last the sheriff arrived at the staging area. Jack glanced at his watch. Past three o'clock already—not much daylight left. Lieutenant Oxford spotted Jack's patrol car and waved him forward. Sporting a broad grin, Madge guided her boss to a prime parking spot adjacent to the trailhead.

"Well, you're dressed for it anyway," she commented on the sheriff's cold-weather outfit as he shut the Charger down, stepped out, and locked the door.

"Right lake, wrong pew," Jack sighed as he allowed himself one final internal lament. Then he put his thoughts of fishing and parties on hold, zipped up his parka, and focused on the task at hand. "Are we walkin' or ridin' down? Please tell me we're ridin'."

"We're riding," said Madge. "The snowmobile crew will be back up pretty soon to give us a lift. They just took Doc down for a look."

"So, Doc's down there?" Jack smiled. "And I'm guessing our young assistant coroner is *not* dressed for this weather."

"I felt sorry for her and lent her a parka and the boys found her some gloves and snow pants, and it took some doing to find something to cover her feet. Serves her right to freeze a toe or two—what's up with a grown woman wearing sneakers in December?"

"And not just any sneakers, I'll bet," said Jack. "I'll wager she was wearin' those little French numbers—one red and one blue—those souvenir sneakers she picked up on her trip to Europe—the ones she's always goin' on about. That gal's still nostalgic for France. What's next? A beret? More of that crazy French underwear?" The sheriff paused because Madge was staring at him with a curious expression. "What?" he asked.

"Too much information," Madge whispered.

Despite the cold, Jack blushed. Madge was right. He needed to be more discrete. Rumors of his relationship with Tiff Northbridge, the county's vivacious young medical examiner, were already swirling around the stationhouse. And his tendency to protest too much where the attractive pathologist was concerned only added fuel to the gossip. He was about to change the subject when the whine of snowmobile engines reached his ears.

"Hmm," he said, "those boys are comin' up a little hot don't you think?"

Stepping back from the trailhead, the sheriff and his lieutenant were fortunate to move aside just as two snowmobiles emerged from the tree-lined trail and burst into view. Racing in single file, the machines moved in harmony—like a pair of synchronized swimmers. Carving a sweeping arc around the staging area, both drivers did wide, one-eighty turns causing each of their droning machines to spew rooster-tails of snow high into the air. As the pair came to a stop and throttled down, an avalanche of white debris trailed behind them and landed on the hood and windshield of Jack's parked patrol car.

"Sorry, Sheriff," said the nearest driver, his face hidden by his visor and ninja gaiter. His voice was sincere, even if muffled by the confines of his snow helmet.

"Sorry," added his companion. "But they said to hurry."

"There's hurry," said Jack, "and then there's bat-crazy snow-speedin'. Well, you're here now so let's get on down to the lake. But take it easy and remember we ain't wearin' helmets."

"I can get you one," said the driver.

"Claustrophobic," said Jack, tapping his head as he declined the offer. "My watch cap and hood will do me just fine. I'll ride down with you while your pal here gets a helmet lid for Madge."

"Thanks," said Madge. "I didn't know you cared."

"You're welcome," Jack grinned as he climbed on behind the nearest snowmobiler, cinched-up the hood of his parka, put on his sunglasses, and tapped the driver on the shoulder. "Let's you and me go down," he instructed the driver. "And take your dang time. It ain't likely the deceased is goin' anywhere."

Chapter 2

Geese

(December 30 / Afternoon)

"Can I look now?" Annie Sands was allowing her husband of six months to steer her through the farmhouse's front door, across the porch, and down the stairs.

"Careful on these steps," Trinidad said. "But keep the blindfold on until you reach the driveway. Trust me, it's a little snowy out here, but I won't let you fall."

"I'm not afraid of falling," she assured him with an impatient whisper. "But I can hear people snickering."

"Shh!" A voice sounded somewhere in front of her.

Despite this admonition, the snickering continued, and Annie could hear voices calling for silence, with each *shush* followed by a chorus of suppressed giggles.

"Either—" Annie scowled as she stopped at the base of the stairs and refused to go further. "Either my unscrupulous detective of a conniving husband has conspired with others to fill our driveway with a flock of unruly geese—either that or my scheming spouse has disobeyed my strict instructions. I distinctly said no celebrating my birthday—no party of any kind—and especially no surprise party."

"I don't remember hearing any such instructions," said Trinidad. "That is, I may have heard something like that, but I definitely *was not* listening. Anyhow, come on—we're almost there," he whispered as he gently urged his bride to continue walking.

"I'm freezing," said one of the geese.

"Oh, for pity sakes," said another. "Let the birthday girl have a look!"

"Now you've done it!" scolded yet another voice.

"Surprise!" shouted a ragged chorus, compelling Trinidad to remove Annie's blindfold.

Opening her eyes, Annie was momentarily blinded by the sparkle of winter sunshine glinting off the surface of freshly-fallen snow. The young woman had to blink repeatedly to take in the farmyard scene. As her eyes adjusted, she counted twenty members of the Lavender community standing before her—every citizen bundled against the cold, and all lined up across the driveway. To the puzzled woman it seemed as if more than half of the tiny village's wintertime population had managed to assemble at Lavender Hill Farm without her knowledge. By whatever means the crowd had materialized, a tight row of familiar faces stood shoulder-to-shoulder in the broad driveway of the newlyweds' rural acreage. It was an unexpected gathering, and, to her astonished eyes, the group looked like a ragged rank of soldiers—a military formation poised to charge onto a cold-weather battlefield, or perhaps assembled to play the part of an impatient firing squad.

The only things missing are muskets and bayonets, she told herself.

As if to reinforce Annie's warlike notions, Trinidad left his new bride to face the crowd alone and literally marched toward the center of the row of community members where he did a military about-face and grinned back at his confused wife.

"Open ranks please," said Trinidad and the assembled citizens side-stepped to reveal what their tightly-knit line had been hiding. Their parting maneuver exposed a sight which left Annie staring in amazement as she beheld a powder-blue Mini Cooper sitting in the farm's snowbound driveway with an enormous tangle of red satin ribbons balanced on the little car's roof.

"Well, you should say something," Trinidad prompted.

"I don't—" Annie stammered. "Where—? I—this is really too much—I had no idea they came in that color—I mean you really shouldn't have—"

"I meant, you should say something comprehensible," Trinidad suggested.

"Oh you," she said as she rushed forward to first punch her husband in the shoulder and then embrace him—holding him tightly for fifty heartbeats.

"Aw," someone gushed.

"Happy birthday!" the crowd shouted. Then its disparate members gathered around the couple and erupted into a completely unintelligible version of the traditional birthday song—their discordant voices forming clouds of frost in the frigid air.

"I was right," said Annie and she laughed heartily while the disjointed chorus mangled words and music. "I knew I heard geese."

"Never mind our singing," said Father Thomas. "I've heard much worse on any given Sunday. Now, for the love of Heaven, girl, will you please jump in and start this infernal machine so we can all applaud and cheer and then go inside and get warm?"

Chapter 3

Birthday

(December 30 / Afternoon)

As the birthday celebration filled Lavender Hill's cozy farmhouse with music and conversation, Trinidad stood in the hallway and hung up the phone.

"I told my eager-beaver husband not to get a landline." Annie laughed from the kitchen where she and a neighbor lady were heating more cocoa and apple cider. "The telemarketers have us zeroed in like a platoon of troublesome Nazis with well-calibrated mortars."

"You're aware that your married name—you must know that 'Sands' is German," said Mrs. Liberstein with a disapproving frown.

"I meant Nazis, not Germans," said Annie. "There's a difference, right?"

"If you say so, dear," answered Mrs. Liberstein. "If you say so," she emphatically repeated the observation, reinforcing the possibility that she was skeptical of the younger woman's logic.

"Sorry, Caroline. My only excuse is it's my birthday," Annie apologized. "And I've been hitting the cider."

"The cider's not spiked, dear," said Mrs. Liberstein. "But don't you mind this old woman. I'm just glad my late husband isn't alive to hear you making light of the Nazis. He had very strong opinions on the Nazis."

"Don't we all?" Annie agreed. "I wish I had a nickel for every time I heard about some horror perpetrated by the dastardly Third Reich."

"A nickel," said Mrs. Liberstein, her voice pensive.

So poignant was the older woman's tone and so distant the look which clouded Caroline Liberstein's eyes, that Annie stared at her and would have asked a question. But the birthday girl was distracted when she caught a glimpse of Trinidad who, like Caroline, seemed to be also lost in thought.

"Who was it, Honey?" Annie asked with a note of concern in her voice.

Trinidad was leaning against the kitchen wall. He seemed to need it for support.

"Herb Schulz is dead," he said.

"What?" asked Annie.

"Dead," Mrs. Liberstein mumbled as she struggled to her feet and then immediately sunk back into her chair, seemingly stricken by the news.

"Somebody just said old man Schulz is dead!" Father Thomas shouted as he rushed into the kitchen.

"Who says he's dead?" demanded Burt Loop who trailed the minister.

Soon the kitchen was packed with partygoers all talking at once and all asking the same questions. Trinidad pulled Annie aside.

"It looks like murder and the county dispatcher says Jack wants me up on the Mesa," he whispered. "I'm sorry. I know it's your party and all, but I need to go help him out."

"What party?" asked Annie. "Who said anything about a frigging party?"

Trinidad hesitated, unable to determine if his bride of six months was or was not angry.

"Go," Annie said. "Jack needs a detective apparently—and he's asking for you—*not us*. So, go on—go play private eye. Besides I need to stay and take care of Caroline who looks as if she's seen a ghost—plus I've still got a mob of geese in here to feed and water."

Chapter 4

Dry-Bag
(December 30 / Afternoon)

Alone in the upstairs master bedroom, Trinidad opened the closet door and reached up to grasp the dangling end of the pull-chain.

Got to rewire that switch, he reminded himself for the hundredth time as an awkward tug on the stubborn chain ignited the single naked bulb which dangled precariously from the high ceiling. Annie had been after him to replace the wonky closet light with a more elegant arrangement of a fashionable globe and a practical wall switch. He made a mental note to visit Big John's Ace Hardware in Cedaredge and pick up the necessary parts—one of these days when he was in town.

Meanwhile, knowing it would be much colder on top of Grand Mesa, the detective grabbed his parka, gloves, and snow boots. Then he turned and crossed the room to array his gear on the bed. He stood for a moment, convinced he was forgetting something.

"Hmm," he said aloud. Returning to the closet, he searched the shelves until he located a scarf and pair of gaiters. To reach the gaiters, he had to shove aside the colorful drybag which protruded from the lower shelf. There wouldn't be time to unseal the bag before he drove up to Island Lake, but he'd deal with it when he returned. He switched off the light, closed the closet door, and bundled up.

Downstairs, he said his goodbyes to the assembled guests, accepted a surprising hug from Caroline Liberstein, and disappointed the family dog by telling her she'd have to stay.

"Sorry, Cozy," Trinidad told the eager shepherd. "Not today."

"You sure took your sweet time upstairs getting ready," Annie frowned.

"When I say I'll be ready in ten minutes," Trinidad said, "even *I* don't believe it."

"Kiss," Annie requested.

"Roger that," Trinidad complied.

Outside, he studied the sky for a moment before crossing to the shed and forcing the rolling door open.

Something else to fix, he reminded himself.

He started his Honda Ridgeline, backed out, put the Honda in park, got out to close the shed door, and returned to the driver's seat. Passing by the cars and trucks which the party-goers had concealed in a snowy grove just beyond the corrals, Trinidad smiled thinking how neatly he'd pulled off Annie's surprise celebration—a logistical triumph considering how rapidly rumors were apt to spread in the Village of Lavender. For a change, apparently, nobody had talked—or probably they had talked plenty among themselves and yet no one had divulged the secret to the birthday girl.

"Secrets," Trinidad said the word aloud as he put the Ridgeline in four-wheel-drive and started up the snowbound hill which led to the farm's now-dormant lavender fields.

Certainly, Herbert Schulz had his secrets, the majority of which had resided for months at Lavender Hill Farm in the upstairs closet. As Trinidad reached the top of the hill and passed through the sleeping fields, he recalled the stormy morning, months ago, when Herbert had arrived at the farmhouse door, in the rain, clutching the dry-bag to his breast.

On that day, it was gloriously wet, the air was clean and crisp, and the lavender fields were resplendent in all their bluish-purple glory.

"Going on a river trip?" the detective asked his visitor as he eyed the highway-orange bag.

"I prefer my water frozen," Herbert quipped. "I'd sure rather skate on ice than ride a bucking bronco of a whitewater raft and get splashed in the face for my trouble. Not to mention soaking my underpants."

"Can't argue with you there," Trinidad laughed. "So, my friend, come on in. I'll make some coffee and you can tell me what's in the bag."

The two men sat at the kitchen table, drinking coffee, and shooting the breeze. Herbert was in the village on one of his periodic visits to get supplies and check his mailbox. Otherwise, as Trinidad and everyone in Lavender knew, the old man spent most of his days, in all seasons, rain or shine, in his Grand Mesa cabin.

While the young man and the elder spoke, the dry-bag remained in one of the otherwise vacant chairs—unmentioned and unopened. The detective knew that the unique bag was specially designed for use by outdoor enthusiasts. The water-tight fabric featured sturdy sides, a secure bottom, and a tightly-sealed top to protect its contents from moisture. He glanced once at the bag, then once more, but—when it became clear that Herbert wasn't going to satisfy his host's curiosity—Trinidad focused his attention on his visitor. So, the bag literally sat there, an inanimate object, occupying its own chair, and naturally mute. Nevertheless, as the morning advanced and the men talked, Trinidad couldn't shake the irrational impression that the bag seemed to be listening.

After three cups of coffee and an hour's rambling conversation, Herbert grinned and steered the topic back to his mysterious bag.

"I suppose you're wondering," the old man casually suggested, "what's in yonder bag."

"The thought had crossed my mind," Trinidad admitted. "Criss-crossed it in fact—about two hundred times."

"Well—" Herbert began, then paused as a crimson patina spread across his wrinkled face. "The truth is you'll probably be disappointed to know it falls quite short of the treasure which the Lavender gossips believe I've been hoarding all these years."

"So, it ain't the fortune in rare stamps, gold doubloons, Anastasia's lost jewelry, or valuable baseball cards that the village rumor-mill has speculated?"

"Not even close," Herbert admitted. "See for yourself."

In the end, the bag contained what turned out to be the very thing Trinidad had anticipated. Others may not have thought of old Herbert Schulz as a writer, but the detective was unsurprised. The man was literate, that much was evident by his conversation—which was always a notch above the local themes of weather and crops, spectator sports, and hunting and fishing. So, it seemed only natural that Herbert had produced an autobiographical manuscript.

At Herbert's request, Trinidad had begun reading the manuscript, had meant to read more, but—like a lot of the detective's best intentions—that promise had remained unfulfilled.

"Something else to fix," he said aloud as he left his farm fields behind, steered onto the county road, and headed toward the highway. "And too late now—too darn late."

Chapter 5

The Usual
(December 30 / 4:20 p.m.)

It was still light when Trinidad reached the Island Lake staging area and found the usual crime scene personalities assembled there. The snowbound clearing on the bluff near the trailhead was occupied by three forensic technicians along with two paramedics, a cluster of uniformed officers, a photographer, and the perky new assistant coroner. Tiff Northbridge seemed a bit out of place, but she was clearly the center of attention. Drinking coffee from a Styrofoam cup, she stood next to a blazing fire barrel surrounded by a semi-circle of men, all gazing at her adoringly. Like most other men, Trinidad could certainly appreciate what Jack Treadway saw in her.

The newly-arrived detective nodded in Tiff's direction. The young woman gave a shrug and gestured at her audience as if to say, look at all these brave boys. Trinidad might have crossed the clearing then, but he decided not to mingle. Knowing he was an interloper among these dedicated public servants, the detective stayed put and merely acknowledged the crew with a wave of his hand.

Tiff waved back, the others didn't.

The assembled group represented law enforcement's absolutely essential supporting cast of characters and Trinidad was amazed that so many had been called to the Mesa during what he knew to be a county holiday. Such a healthy response, he surmised, was a tribute to the lead actors in this little winter's day drama. All these people were here, not only out of a sense of civic duty, but also as an expression of loyalty to his good friend Jack and the sheriff's faithful lieutenant.

As for the whereabouts of those two principal actors, Trinidad decided that Sheriff Jack Treadway and Lieutenant Madge Oxford must be down at the lake, along with some of the big-city lab boys from Grand Junction. It stood to reason that the Junction-based Colorado Bureau of Investigation would be putting their oar in. So, the CBI was probably somewhere around, and the U.S. Forest Service wouldn't be far behind, although Trinidad knew their enforcement crew was stretched thin. To round out the scene, there was also a ubiquitous food truck on the premises, as well as a portable convenience in case anybody needed to use the john. Everyone had a job to do, and Trinidad recognized that all the people up here and those down below at the frozen lake would be acting their parts and playing essential roles in the drama of what he presumed would be a homicide investigation.

Just what role a private detective like himself would be enacting was anybody's guess.

In any event, the usual team was on hand and, given the season and depth of the snow, it came as no surprise that this afternoon's cast was augmented by the presence of several snowmobilers. An array of powerful trucks and lengthy trailers lined the highway side of the staging area. A cluster of snowmobiles and their warmly-bundled operators formed a ragged line nearby and Trinidad guessed a handful more would be down at the lake below. Deciding to leave the professionals to themselves and mingle instead with other civilians, the curious detective walked in the direction of the snowmobilers.

Trinidad waved a friendly hand toward the assembled snowmobiles. He was searching for a familiar face—a bit of a challenge considering everybody was bundled up. Seeing none, he assumed the group didn't include anyone from the village.

More likely, he told himself, *this is a Delta City club.*

Nevertheless, he walked closer and got eye-contact with one of the riders. The rider sat astride his vehicle wearing a brightly colored snowsuit and helmet. His hood was down, and he had one ear to a two-way radio, apparently awaiting orders. As Trinidad approached, the man held up a finger, said something into the radio, then set the instrument aside.

"A busy night," the detective suggested.

"You got that right," the rider answered. "We're busy hauling personnel and equipment. And law-dogs."

"And a fox," quipped another rider who nodded in the direction of the food truck.

"Yeah, a fox," agreed his mate who also turned his attention that way.

Trinidad followed their earnest stares and saw the source of their "fox" comment.

Tiff Northbridge was in their sights as she held court on the far side of the clearing. Still surrounded by a gaggle of men, the effervescent young woman was looking radiant despite her bulky parka which failed to conceal her unmistakable allure. Seeing Trinidad, she caught his eye and made a subtle motion which he interpreted as a cry for help. He could relate. Some people—women and men also—had a tendency to view the detective as handsome and to focus on his looks, discounting any other skills and talents he might possess. He imagined it was probably that way for Tiff too, if not more so. Feeling suddenly gallant, Trinidad crossed to the food truck, ordered some coffee, and said hello to Tiff. She said hello back.

"Everything okay?" he whispered.

"Peachy," she whispered.

Assuming he'd misinterpreted her situation, Trinidad started back. He was halfway across the clearing when he heard swift footfalls crunching on the snow and turned to see Tiff hastening to join him. He waited as she moved rapidly, each step a struggle to keep her balance in a pair of snow boots which were several sizes too big. Breathless from her sudden dash through the snow, she caught hold of his arm.

"I need to be rescued," she panted.

"From—?" Trinidad prompted.

"Everyone," she said. "I've got a lot to do. I've got reports to write and I can't get a lick of work done with all these men orbiting around."

Of course, the men are orbiting—they know a heavenly body when they see one, Trinidad told himself. But he had enough sense to suppress that chauvinistic thought and said aloud, "Can't you hide out in your car?"

"I'm nearly out of gas," she admitted. "And I'd freeze in my car without the dome light on and the heater and engine running."

"Here," said Trinidad and he handed over the keys to his Honda Ridgeline. "You can fire-up my beast and run the lights and heater all you like—I've got plenty of gas."

"Thanks," she said. "You're an angel. I'll get my briefcase."

Left alone while Tiff occupied his vehicle, Trinidad found time to return his thoughts to Herbert Schulz. The old man's death had been unexpected. Though the initial shock was wearing off, the detective was still processing the aftermath, especially his own feelings of remorse and regret. He could have been a better friend, should have kept his promises. Herbert was gone, and all Trinidad could manage now was trying to do better going forward.

Bloom where you're planted—that was something Herbert was fond of saying. Starting tonight, Trinidad would do what he could to honor the old man's memory, which included taking time to read the deceased's autobiography and, if possible, striving to reconcile his loss by helping Jack and the others achieve a sense of justice.

The dispatcher's call to the farmhouse had been vague about details, but the implication was that foul play was suspected. At the very least, it was an unattended death, which meant an investigation was in order. The detective would know more when Jack summoned him to the lake. In the meantime, Trinidad considered what he knew about Herbert Schulz.

Herbert was in his nineties although he looked and acted younger. Still, it was common knowledge that he'd been an adolescent during World War II so, whatever his true age, most people thought it was just a matter of time before the reclusive man turned up dead.

Living alone, year-round, in the relative wilderness of Grand Mesa would be a challenge for a younger man, let alone the county's elder statesman. There were plenty of hazards for an older individual to contend with. Bears, of course, but the weather was the main threat. Herbert wasn't one to just hole-up in his cabin. Even in the depths of winter, cross-country skiers regularly encountered the old man, far from civilization—usually snowshoeing and often tethered to a sled laden with gear or food or firewood. He was fit for his age—fit for any age. He was a survivor, although only a select few knew the dimensions of his survival story.

Trinidad counted himself among those who knew at least the broad outline of Herbert's background. Jack also knew some of Herbert's story. As for the details, the detective once again chided himself for failing to read the whole of the old man's manuscript. Still, he knew enough to recognize the irony of Herbert's death. Had Herbert survived a world war to end his days in the Colorado mountains? Did the old man foresee his fate? Herbert's writing was packed with premonitions.

"Give it a read," Herbert had requested on that rainy day when he'd entrusted his manuscript to Trinidad. "I know you're busy, but I'd appreciate hearing your impressions."

Trinidad had promised to get it done, but he was only a quarter of the way through the old man's manuscript when life as a consulting detective got complicated. Faced with a series of domestic and investigative challenges, he put the manuscript back inside the dry-bag, re-sealed the thing, stuck it in the closet, and promptly forgot it.

Someone's car alarm tripped, and the strident sound pulled Trinidad back to the present. Uttering a string of profanities, one of the snowmobilers scurried toward his truck. A series of chirps and the alarm was subdued. The detective ordered another cup of coffee, drank it down, and warmed his hands at the fire barrel.

He was beginning to think Jack had forgotten him until he heard two snowmobiles working their way up from the lake. With the noise of their approach echoing among the snowbound trees, the machines pounded through the darkness with a beat so regular that they seemed to be moving in rhythm.

The snowmobilers were on a steep snowbound trail which ascended from the broad expanse of Island Lake below to reach the bluff on which the detective and the others stood. The trail was a primitive pathway about as wide as a city sidewalk. Trinidad had traveled that distance many times and in all seasons. He knew the route sliced through a narrow break in the thick pine forest. It would be a rather ordinary hike in daylight and fair weather but a challenge to traverse on snow and in the gathering darkness.

As the yet-unseen machines grew nearer, there could be no doubt as to their destination. Although still distant, the sound of a pair of laboring engines grew ever louder, and two headlamp beams sent shafts of illumination up through the dark trees. To Trinidad, the quavering beams resembled searchlights crisscrossing a nighttime sky to beckon film buffs to the cinematic premiere of an alpine movie.

Annie and her cinematic passions, he thought. *She's definitely getting to me.*

His thoughts about his new bride's love for the cinema were interrupted as the snowmobiles emerged from the dense trees. Arriving in single file, each in turn topped the snow trail and burst into view, puncturing the chilly mountain air with an abrupt bang—as penetrating as a cannon shot. The noise mounted as the conveyances zoomed across the clearing. Momentary echoes reverberated in the growing darkness, only to instantly fade to an abrupt silence when both machines came to a stop near a hauler trailer and simultaneously shut down.

In the sudden quiet, Trinidad watched the riders push their vehicles a short distance, each footstep crunching in the frozen snow. He watched also as each man rubbed down his mount and loaded his machine into the hauler. The snowmobiles were piloted by helmeted drivers, who'd undoubtedly been recruited from the ranks of winter sports enthusiasts who frequent the lofty Mesa. Their role at present was to ferry men, women, and equipment between this staging area next to Highway 65 and the lake below. When the hauler departed, the detective realized he was witnessing a shift change. Sensing it would soon be his turn to journey to the lake, Trinidad crossed the staging area to make use of the so-called *teahouse*—that was law enforcement's somewhat civilized and mostly satirical name for what was officially referred to as a *chemical toilet*. His duty completed, he grabbed another cup of coffee, sat with the paramedics on the bumper of their ambulance, and waited for transport.

While the detective lingered, the last hint of daylight faded. At this altitude, on a clear night, the stars would be spectacular. But the Mesa was socked in, and tonight's waxing crescent moon would offer no illumination. So, it would soon be pitch dark on Island Lake's frozen surface and, by now, only a few people would be left down there. It was growing later and colder but—knowing what he would find below—Trinidad was in no hurry to reach the lake. He took one last look at the staging scene before the coming darkness overwhelmed it. He had the feeling that, once he went down and returned again, all this would be gone.

To create this artificially broad space in the deep snow, plows had been enlisted to gouge out a flat clearing. The resulting site sat adjacent to the intersection of the well-groomed highway and the narrower snowbound service road which encircled Island Lake. All that work had taken time which caused Trinidad to wonder how many hours had passed after Herbert had been discovered and who'd found the body. He'd ask Jack when he saw him—if he ever managed to reach the lake. His being there at all was beginning to feel superfluous.

Fully aware that his presence was incidental to the official work of law enforcement, the detective decided to sooth his bruised ego by honing his observational skills. He wasn't quite certain why, but it seemed important—before it all vanished—to make a final mental inventory of vehicles occupying the staging area. There was the ambulance where he sat, the nearby cluster of snowmobile trailers, and the food truck—which seemed to be packing up. In addition, the clearing held two patrol cars—Jack's and the lieutenant's he presumed. Near the sheriff's vehicles was Tiff's SUV and Trinidad's own Honda along with a fire rescue vehicle, two highway department trucks, and two civilian sedans and an unmarked truck. Presumably, these extra vehicles were meant to be there and presumably, on this snowbound night, they were all equipped with four-wheel-drive.

The occupants of these diverse vehicles were milling about, but only Tiff and the highway workers seemed busy. Clad in reflective gear, the highway crew was actively manning barricades to ensure that the evening's highway traffic—however infrequent at night and in the dead of winter—came nowhere near the staging area. As for Tiff, the temperature was dropping, and Trinidad's Honda Ridgeline was emitting a vapory skein of exhaust which trailed out into the darkening night. He could see the beautiful young woman sitting in the cab—her parka now removed to reveal her red sweater, shimmering blonde hair, and cherubic face. It was a bright tableau highlighted by the Ridgeline's dashboard lights and overhead lamp. He sensed that every other man in the staging area was also attracted to Tiff's illuminated profile as they stomped their booted feet, crowded around fire barrels, and tried to stay warm.

Moths to the flame, he thought, seeking to remind himself that he was a married man.

As the detective contemplated Tiff's visage from fifty feet away, a new trailer arrived, whereupon two more snowmobiles were off-loaded and fired up. Moments later, one of the riders signaled for Trinidad.

"Body still down there?" Trinidad asked as he mounted the rear seat of a candy-apple red snowmobile. From what the detective knew of law enforcement procedure, delays in moving a body were not uncommon. One sticking point, he supposed, was Tiff's role in approximating time of death—an estimate which would surely be complicated by winter temperatures.

"Far as I know," said the driver. "Although, with all that's goin' on, they could've drug five stiffs outa here without I would even know it. Beggin' pardon, I hear they say you know the guy. Sorry. Anyway, I'm relieving the crew what hauled a crap-load of lights down there earlier. Looks like the fuzz is planning to spend the night—uh—no offense."

"I'm not a uniform," said Trinidad.

"Can't tell with you all bundled up. Smart to be dressed warm though. It's only gonna get colder now that sundown's here. You want a helmet?"

"Absolutely," said Trinidad who was thinking about how Jack's unexpected call was about to oblige Lavender's daunting detective to plummet down a dark and snowy trail to reach the icy environs of a high-altitude alpine lake. "I've got a wife at home who would be very upset with me if I managed to scramble what brains I have left," Trinidad added.

"I hear you, pal," said the driver. "Cinch this up good and hang on."

The ride down was invigorating. Despite the obvious hazard of having to negotiate it in the dark, the path had been well-groomed by the evening's heavy traffic and the way down was surprisingly broad. The snowmobile's headlamp provided ample traveling lights and the detective only had to duck twice to avoid contact with low-hanging tree branches.

When his ride reached the bottom of the pathway, the driver moved aside to yield to another snowmobile which was about to head up. When the machines came abreast, the ascending passenger held up a hand, halting both vehicles.

"Welcome aboard," Madge's familiar voice echoed in her helmet.

"Lieutenant," Trinidad grinned. "How'd you recognize me?"

"Your coming was foretold," said Madge as she waggled a radio in the detective's direction.

"Understood," said Trinidad.

"Well, gotta run," said Madge. "Good hunting."

"Good hunting," Trinidad responded with the standard law enforcement tagline.

Madge held on as her driver gunned the snowmobile and headed uphill. Trinidad did the same as his driver started across the frozen surface of Island Lake. As the snowmobile gathered speed, the detective glimpsed a cluster of lights in the near distance. Apparently, the crime scene was not far but the snowmobiler was approaching the lights obliquely, taking a wide arc, presumably to avoid a direct line. The snug-fitting helmet conspired with Trinidad's parka and cap to muffle his ears, but he could still hear the faint chugging sound of a portable generator. Soon, he detected the shimmering movement of yellow crime tape, and it was clear the snowmobile was on a path which avoided that barrier. The wide turn continued, and the detective tucked his head behind the driver to keep the freezing air from taking his breath.

As they drew closer to the lights, Trinidad recognized that the yellow tape formed a makeshift boundary which lined two sides of an extended rectangle about as long as a squeeze-chute which ranchers used to move cattle out of a holding pen and into a loading truck. The plastic borderline was tethered to metal fence posts which someone, using God knows what process, had managed to hammer into the ice. When at last they reached the tape, the detective's driver turned sharply and brought his snowmobile to a halt outside the perimeter.

"This is as far as I get," the man said. "You want I should wait? Or should I go up top again and you'll call me down on the radio?"

"You might as well go up and keep warm. I'm not sure how long I'll be," said Trinidad. He handed the helmet back and watched the man reach around to secure the headgear behind the driver's seat, using the passenger restraint strap and what looked like a sling. The man looked up when he felt the detective's gaze and opened his visor to reveal a handsome freckled face which, despite the darkness and the cold, seemed to glow with something approaching angelic light.

"It's the harness for my kid," the jolly man explained. "Keeps the little bugger from sliding off and it's handy for tying other stuff down too. If something falls off out here, we can forget about it 'til Spring—which is curious now that I think about it."

"How's that?" asked Trinidad who was in no hurry to duck under the crime scene tape.

"Well, the word is that this fella down here was shot and left out on the ice—" the man paused and looked up from his task, perhaps thinking he was talking out of turn.

"Go on—" Trinidad prompted.

"Well," said the man, "I ain't no detective, but it seems to me—if a fella was going to go to all the trouble to shoot a guy way out here in the middle of no place—then why not ditch the body in a snowbank? That way it'd be months before he showed. Why leave him out here on the ice to be spotted so easy? It's almost like as if the shooter wanted us to find him. Am I figuring this right?"

"Couldn't have figured it better myself," Trinidad said, and the detective smiled as he shook hands with the insightful snowmobiler.

Chapter 6

On Ice
(December 30 / 5:45 p.m.)

Trinidad Sands had seen his share of dead bodies, but there was something fundamentally disheartening about viewing the icy tarp which covered Herbert Schulz's mortal remains. Beneath that thin canvas—splayed out on the ice—lay Herbert's lifeless body, forlorn and abandoned with no one to mourn him. No sooner had Trinidad considered this morbid thought than he amended it.

No one to mourn his passing except Caroline Liberstein of course and the man's numberless friends. I should be fortunate to be so missed when I'm gone. And I'll miss him too because he was a friend, Trinidad told himself.

As a cold wind crept across the mirrored surface of Island Lake, the detective's thoughts turned to the last time he'd seen the old man alive.

Only last week, he and Herbert had been sitting in the cozy confines of the Village of Lavender Pancake House. The weather outside was unseasonably warm and, rather than snow, the day had seen a steady drizzle of icy rain. The unlikely pair occupied their favorite booth which offered an unobstructed view of the place's parking lot and the distant outline of Grand Mesa. They had just finished ordering breakfast when Herbert drew his young companion's attention to an SUV which was passing slowly through the lot.

"That's a tourist for certain," Herbert laughed.

"Yet another stranger who got caught in the muddy clutches of Old Goat Trail," Trinidad grinned as he remembered the summer of 2018, when Annie—then a stranger—and her little mud-covered Volkswagen bug had rolled into his life. On that day, the VW's wheel wells, tires, and undercarriage had been caked with a patina of caramel-colored mud. The lower margins of the dark SUV were similarly discolored.

"Two guesses where he's headed," Herbert said.

"The car wash of course," Trinidad surmised. "Been there, done that."

"Notice anything else peculiar about that rig, Mr. Detective?" the older man asked.

Trinidad turned in his seat.

"Unless I'm mistaken," Trinidad said, "there was no front license plate. Can't read the rear one for the mud, but I'm guessing Arizona or New Mexico."

"Twenty-one states don't require front plates," Herbert noted. "Something a license plate collector like me knows for certain. So, it could be anyplace from Alabama to West Virginia—but I've got to agree with your deduction. Most likely it's a Four Corners car. Not many faraway visitors come up this way in winter."

They watched the Toyota for a few moments more, then returned to their conversation. That morning's theme was a familiar one as Herbert related yet another of his intriguing war stories. As far as the ninety-four-year-old veteran was concerned, World War II was not a distant memory. The war was something he carried with him every day of his life, along with the eternal memory of his dear departed wife. Over the years, Herbert's conversations with Trinidad had touched on both topics with equal feeling.

Meeska Schulz, Herbert's German-born war-bride of sixty years, had died more than a decade ago. Trinidad had met her several times, near the end of her life. He recalled her as a gracious individual who was intelligent and witty, and—thanks to Herbert's vivid memories—the detective was privileged to learn even more about the fascinating woman.

"Every morning—" Herbert would say as he paused for breath and also to master his emotions. "Every morning, she had fresh flowers in the bowl on the kitchen table. Rain or shine and summer or winter—it didn't matter. Drought or downpour, the same. Always the flowers, every morning. How did she do it? I ask you, how did she do it?"

Trinidad would sit in silence as the old man wiped a tear away and laboriously blew his bulbous red nose. Then the detective would say, "A remarkable woman."

"That she was," Herbert would agree. "That she was."

Herbert had landed at Normandy in June 1944. On the beach, he took a bullet in the forearm, fell, and was momentarily trapped beneath an avalanche of bodies as wave after wave of murderous enemy fire felled his comrades. On his feet again, he fought his way inland, survived the Battle of the Bulge, and crossed the Rhine into Germany. Which is where he met Meeska.

On patrol, he heard sobbing. Digging through rubble, he discovered a petite German girl and pulled her from the bombed-out wreckage of a Remagen bakery. The instant he rescued the frightened seventeen-year-old, she put her thin arms around the solid nineteen-year-old soldier's thick neck. He recalled that she was light as a feather when he carried her to an aid station where she continued to cling to him, refusing to let go while they examined her. Nor would she surrender the small sketchpad she held tightly in one delicate hand.

"Nothing wrong with this girl," the Army surgeon had pronounced. "Except I think probably she's in love with her liberator."

Herbert's halting German, mostly kitchen phrases learned from his paternal grandmother, was rusty. But he managed to communicate his sudden uncommon affection for the distraught girl, and he promised to write to her and return for her. She seemed to understand and carefully printed a mailing address on a sheet of drawing paper—the number and street of the house of her uncle in Berlin. He did the same, hastily scrawling his parents' Grand Junction address in Meeska's sketchpad.

Then the war parted them.

With Europe liberated, his outfit had been on a troopship steaming through the Panama Canal and bound for the Pacific Theater when Japan surrendered.

"They turned us right around and brought us home," he reminisced. "Right over to Galveston, then the gangplank came down and there we were—back in the land of the living."

For months after the war ended the love-sick soldier had tried to correspond with the lovely Meeska. At first, their letters must have crossed in the mail because no word reached either during the closing days of 1945. Eventually the occupying forces established Allied Mail in divided Germany. Meeska's letters came pouring in and at last Herbert had a conduit to write to her. The couple had kept all the letters—both sides of the correspondence—and, as the years of their married life passed, he and his wife had been fond of reading them aloud to one another—a tradition which kept their love strong and their romance fresh.

"Such a love," Annie exclaimed when Trinidad told his new bride of the Schulz's ritual.

Herbert and Meeska had been married by proxy and the additional paperwork required to bring his beloved war-bride to America in 1946 was surprisingly simple. So simple that, almost before they knew it, the two lovebirds went to work establishing a ranch on his parents' property in Roubidoux Canyon. Decades passed and their surprisingly shiftless sons wandered off, disowning their heritage, and showing absolutely no interest in running the family business.

Too old to work the land and tend the stock, Herbert and his wife sold the Schulz Ranch at auction for a record-breaking sum and the wealthy couple returned to civilization. First, they tried to settle in Delta City, which they found far too noisy. At last, they relocated to the Village of Lavender where they became pillars of the community, donating funds to build a clinic and hire the town's first doctor and dentist, then eventually endowing the town library and purchasing a new engine for Lavender's small volunteer fire department.

They were committed to their new community and also completely devoted to one another. Herbert had always been an active outdoorsman and Meeska was his constant companion as the two spry senior citizens explored every inch of the nearby forests of Grand Mesa. In 2009, when Meeska died suddenly, her grieving husband consoled himself by boarding up their village dwelling and improving a remote plot of forest land where he built a rustic cabin, far from civilization.

Friends pleaded with him to return to Lavender, at least for the winter, but he resisted. He remained an avid hiker who had no use for all-terrain-vehicles or snowmobiles, preferring boots in mild weather and cross-country skis and snowshoes when the elevated Mesa became snowbound. Using his own power and with an energy which belied his advancing years, he regularly traversed miles of dense forest, traveling the distance from his cabin to reach a primitive carport where he kept his vintage jeep. He'd drive the jeep to town for supplies and mail and fellowship. After visiting with friends, he'd return to the carport and head back to his cabin.

Although Herbert lived most of the time deep in the woods, and gained a reputation as a hermit, he was no recluse. He kept in constant touch with his adopted community, making the journey into Lavender as regular as clockwork every two weeks to call on acquaintances and acquire supplies. It was during one of the old man's recurring visits that he, Trinidad, and Jack Treadway—none of whom could resist the Pancake House's specialty breakfasts—had first struck up an acquaintance.

When not in Lavender communing with his former neighbors, Herbert had remained alone in his cabin, reading, reminiscing, writing, and—if the rumors are to be believed—possibly coupling with an elderly neighbor who lived on the spread next to Lavender Hill Farm. There were persistent rumors that Caroline Liberstein, also widowed, had hosted Herbert at her farm and had more than once stayed with him out there in the woods. And maybe these circumstances had occurred a bit too often, or so a few wagging tongues suggested. To Trinidad and Annie, his loving bride, the fact that Herbert and Caroline spent time together on her farm and in the wilderness and even shared a bed seemed the most natural thing in the world.

And yet the gossip persisted.

Eventually the talk gave rise to another, even more titillating rumor, putting forth the notion that Herbert was writing a book. When word of this speculation reached Trinidad, nothing could have astonished him less. To the detective, the idea of Herbert as an author seemed as natural as the idea that two senior citizens shared a romantic relationship.

The sound of Jack clearing his throat pulled Trinidad back to the present. He guessed that the sheriff was growing impatient. After greeting the detective, Jack had moved aside to allow Trinidad a moment alone with the body. That moment had stretched into several while Trinidad became immersed in thoughts about his remarkable friend.

Anyone who didn't know Herbert well might wonder what this unique senior citizen was doing out here alone on the ice. Trinidad knew that Herbert had been exceptionally agile for his age and the old man enjoyed remarkable health. During warm seasons he hiked. When summer ended, autumn passed, and winter arrived, Herbert adopted his customary cold-weather routine. In the frosty months, he took to the ice. The vigorous old man had a fondness for skating the width and length of Island Lake. Trinidad surmised that his friend must have been pursuing his winter passion when he was killed.

With effort, the detective sought to shake off memories of the past and turn his attention to the grim task at hand. At last, Trinidad knelt beside the body, lifted the tarp, and saw the damage. Someone had shot Herbert in the back and then, it seemed, had also shot the victim a second time as he lay helpless on the ice. The wounds were diabolical, but not large. Two long-distance shots with a small caliber rifle, he suspected.

"No accident," said the sheriff as he crossed the ice to stand beside the detective.

"Hardly," said Trinidad. "Those two shots couldn't have been more deliberate."

"As for when, it's hard to tell with the temperature," Jack noted. "Tiff—that is Doc Northbridge—estimates sometime late last night or early in the mornin'. I'm goin' with daybreak since I can't see him skatin' in the dark. What do you think, Slick?"

Trinidad didn't answer to the familiar name which Jack had bestowed on him years ago. Instead, he remained in a crouch, gazing sadly at his friend's lifeless body. He placed a hand on Herbert's inert shoulder, said a silent prayer, and repositioned the tarp. Spikes had been driven deep into the ice to keep the canvas in place. Pulling the covering taut, he secured an eyelet to a corner spike and found it difficult to rise. The ice was slick. The detective held up a hand and the sheriff helped him to his feet.

"Given my understanding of Herb's winter habits," Trinidad said, "my guess on the timing would be early this morning."

"Let's go with this mornin' then," Jack agreed.

The detective looked past the covered body where the crime scene tape marked a trail of frozen blood which angled across the ice. "Any other tracks?"

"In addition to the blood path," said Jack, "we found traces of a single pair of ice skates and there's faint evidence that somebody wearin' crampons walked a short distance out onto the ice and went back over their steps—the shooter probably. Otherwise, the ice is windblown and clean as a whistle."

"That figures," said Trinidad. "Any shell casings?"

"You're bound to ask questions which I reckon you already know the answer to," said Jack. "We've got nothin' much down here except the blood track and the body. Up on the shore we found Old Man Schulz's snowshoes, boots, and jacket. And, as for the shoreline snow in that direction, if there'd been any tracks on the trail leadin' down from the bluff, they'd have been erased by the army of snowmobilers who rocketed down here in the a.m. before they spotted the body and then roared back up to report it. So, with few clues to work on, you can see why I called in our famous local detective. Plus, this here's a friend of yours."

"A friend, yes, and I'll help if I can," Trinidad said and then he frowned. "Annie will help too of course, but there's not much to go on and I can't think who'd want to kill such a sweet old guy. Everybody loved him."

"Not everybody," said Jack. "Meanwhile we got a lot less answers than questions."

"Well, I know one question that might surprise you," said Trinidad.

"Which is—" Jack prompted.

"You found Herbert's snowshoes, boots, and jacket, right?"

"Right," Jack confirmed.

"So," said Trinidad, "my question is this: where in the world is Herb's conspicuous wool cap?"

Chapter 7

Body Up
(December 30 / Late)

It was pitch dark when they brought Herbert Schulz's body up from the lake. The ambulance left immediately. The generator and other crime scene paraphernalia were hauled up shortly after. Sheriff Jack Treadway's ride came next. Trinidad Sands lingered on the ice, while his snowmobile taxi idled, then the detective mounted up and followed.

Most of the vehicles in the staging area had dispersed by the time Trinidad and his snowmobile driver followed everyone else uphill. The detective helped the last driver load his machine onto a trailer and watched the man drive away. The highway crews were gone. The place was essentially deserted.

Trinidad was about to head to his own vehicle when he noticed that Tiff Northbridge's SUV was still there with the motor running. Both patrol vehicles were missing which, Trinidad guessed, meant Madge was long gone and Jack had induced somebody to drive his county vehicle back to the station. Which also meant that the sheriff would be riding home with the coquettish medical examiner and the detective wondered if they had enough gas to get there.

Trinidad shook his head. His friend Jack was twenty years older than Tiff, old enough to be her father, so chances were this winter affair of theirs was not going to end well. But who was he to judge? By all accounts, the two were in love and that, the detective decided, was good enough for him.

Determined not to disturb the lovers, Trinidad was making his way across the virtually deserted staging area to reach his Honda Ridgeline when he heard Tiff's SUV backing up and then rolling forward as it slowly crunched over the snow behind him. Trinidad turned and watched as the young woman's car stopped next to him and the passenger-side window rolled down.

"Startin' to snow," said Jack. "Sorry to bring you out on such a night."

"And tell Annie we're sorry we missed the birthday party," yelled Tiff from the driver's seat. The intoxicating scent of her perfume reached Trinidad—an enticing aroma of sandalwood. He felt a twinge of jealousy knowing that these two were undoubtedly headed down the mountain for a night of passionate lovemaking. Tiff had that effect on men, even men like himself who were totally in love with their dear wives.

"I'll tell my intrepid spouse," Trinidad promised. "And, by the way, happy birthday to you too, Tiff. There's a gift for you at the house. Stop by anytime," he added unnecessarily.

"It's something isn't it?" Tiff laughed. "Both me and Annie being December babies and both of us on the 30th. Who knew?"

"Yeah," said Trinidad. "Who knew? So anyway, you two have yourselves a good evening."

"What's left of it," Jack answered. "I'll call you tomorrow."

"But not too early," Tiff called, and Trinidad heard her laugh as Jack rolled up the window and the SUV headed for the highway. Her laughter seemed to echo in the still night and Trinidad decided it would be prudent and neighborly to fire up his Honda and follow them at a discreet distance—just in case they ran out of gas.

The departing SUV's taillights grew smaller, then disappeared in the swirling snow. Walking in total darkness, the detective crossed the unlit staging area to reach his truck. When he opened the driver's side door, he was greeted with the ding-dong rhythm of the keys-left-in-ignition reminder. Tiff had left his keys behind of course, and thank goodness, because otherwise it was a long walk home. To stop the racket, he climbed in and started the Ridgeline. Igniting his lights, he caught a momentary glimpse of movement on the far side of the clearing. He pulled forward just as a dark shape—one of the civilian vehicles he'd noticed earlier—rolled out of the snow-tinged shadows. Trinidad braked and, for an instant, the two vehicles faced one another across the clearing, then the truck—or whatever it was—spun right and silently rolled toward the highway. No engine sound and no lights. So fleeting was the encounter that Trinidad was left wondering if he'd actually seen the other vehicle. By the time he followed, whoever it was had vanished.

Chapter 8

Active Shooter

(December 30 / Late)

After leaving the snowbound clearing at Island Lake behind, Corporal Karl Bistro drove for another five miles in the gathering storm before switching on his headlamps. Mingling at the crime scene had been reckless, but also thrilling and instructive. It had been sufficiently dark and adequately crowded up there so that no one noticed their ranks were infiltrated. As he moved casually among strangers, a few discreetly-worded questions put to those helmeted men who operated the snowmobiles had confirmed that the officials on the scene remained clueless.

Karl decided that the wild card in the mix seemed to be one late-arriving fellow—a tall man with a strong bearing and a dark complexion who kept mostly to himself. That man had been the last to arrive at the clearing and also among the last, along with Karl himself, to leave the mountain. Also, the watchful corporal observed that this distinctive man had apparently volunteered his truck as a working office for the fair-skinned blonde whose illuminated visage captured and held Karl's attention. That sensual distraction had tempted him to remain at the site longer than was prudent. But, in the end, he'd managed to slip away—more-or-less undetected. That was the thrilling part. He'd placed himself squarely in the lion's den, made himself an easy target, if only someone had been on the ball, but no one was. He was in the clear and it was highly probable he'd remain that way.

Karl glanced in his rearview mirror. Even in the falling snow, headlights would be visible. If the wild card Ridgeline was following, that vehicle was too far behind to be a source of worry. In fifteen minutes, Karl would reach the base of the Grand Mesa where scores of side roads intersected with Highway 65—offering a wealth of possible escape routes. More than enough to thwart pursuers, even if he was being pursued and he was confident no one was following. From the highway below, it would require exactly seventeen minutes more to reach his abode—maybe nineteen if the snow kept up. He was certain of his timing. He'd checked and double-checked his calculations. Driving on, he took it easy on the curves. Snow was beginning to accumulate on the steadily descending pavement. His Toyota Tacoma pickup was certainly up to the challenge of winter roads, but becoming stuck on this lofty highway would be much more than inconvenient.

Like clockwork, the efficient corporal rolled down off the Mesa and steered toward home. Precisely eighteen minutes later, he pressed his remote, and guided the Tacoma into the manor's spacious garage. As the bulky steel-reinforced garage door closed behind, Karl glanced at his watch. Perfect timing. He gathered up his rifle, locked the Toyota, and used the keypad to access the manor's stout entry door. He paused at the threshold, as he always did, listening and waiting before he turned on the interior light. Caution, as always, was his by-word.

He centered the rifle on his kitchen table, walked twenty steps to the bar, poured himself a drink, walked back twenty steps, sat down, and waited. At exactly 10:45 p.m. his cellphone pinged with a text message. He typed "Yes" and keyed-in his account number. He didn't bother to respond when his phone pinged again. He knew the transaction was complete, no need to see the confirmation.

Karl downed his drink and set to work breaking-down, cleaning, and reassembling his new JS-2 rifle. Completing that fundamental task, he carried the sleek Chinese weapon to his gun cabinet, punched in the code, secured the firearm in place, and relocked the cabinet door. He took a moment to admire the compact weapon through the thickly-tempered glass. It'd been quite a trick to get the rifle through customs and it had cost him another three thousand to smuggle it in pieces over the Canadian border. Getting his hands on the 5.8-mm ammunition had presented yet another challenge, but it'd been worth all the trouble to obtain the portable, accurate, and—best of all—silent hardware.

Tools of the trade, the corporal thought.

Karl walked back to the bar, counting his steps, and poured himself a second drink. He glanced at the broad bar mirror, portions of which were still spider-webbed with cracks. The damage lingered there as a reminder of the summer morning four months ago when glasses and bottles had been launched in his general direction. The poorly-aimed volley of errant missiles had been hurled by his erstwhile lover during their most recent and final argument. The projectiles had missed their mark and the mirror had become collateral damage, along with his temporary and highly expendable lover. Her fiery temper had ended their turbulent affair and also sealed her fate.

"Redheads," Karl said aloud and for a fleeting moment he wondered how much Judith Delano's flaming auburn hair might have faded by now. What shade would it be? How would those submerged tresses look? What would be the condition of that once-fabulous hair if and when someone managed to fish her body out of the depths of Island Lake—assuming anyone ever did? Contemplating his cracked mirror, he could visualize the turbulent woman as she had once been standing in the room—hands on hips, defiant, and doomed.

He recalled that he'd actually been relieved months ago when Judith had hurled objects while pledging to dissolve their turbulent relationship. Thinking back to that sunny August morning, he'd have been prepared to let her go, if she'd gone quietly. But she tainted her intention to leave by threatening to expose him. In the grip of a fiery tirade, the infuriated redhead vowed to run to the law and divulge all his secrets, disclosing things which he'd foolishly confided in the throes of tempestuous passion. So skilled was her lovemaking and so devious her small mind that Karl had once been tempted to enlist her as a partner. She might have made a passable criminal. Instead, she had become a liability.

Having tossed her poorly-aimed items, the infuriated redhead had stood defiantly in the center of the room, jaw clenched and nostrils flaring. Then she opened her conniving little mouth and launched a verbal assault on her sugar-daddy.

"I've had it," she'd huffed. "It's over and we're done, you motherless weasel! I'm going back to Arizona, but you'd better keep the money coming! Just try cutting me off and see if I don't tell the sheriff, and whoever else will listen, all about your crazy German ideas and your ridiculous nickel fixation! So, even though I love y—"

She'd been on the verge of saying *I love you*—three little words which, in the corporal's vast experience, constituted the Universe's oldest and biggest lie. Although some vague notion of love might have been implied in the emotionally charged atmosphere, Karl's immediate reaction was guided by an entirely different passion. He wasn't motivated by anything resembling affection. Instead, he felt an irresistible sensation of unvarnished fury.

On that fateful day, when Judith's spiteful mouth had formed her last words, they'd been arguing in the manor's den, standing toe-to-toe, like a pair of boxers. So, it was a simple matter for Karl to reach forward, grip the petite woman's fragile throat, and clamp his powerful fingers shut, like the jaws of a varmint trap. When her breath stilled, he released his fatal grip and her lifeless body tumbled to the carpet.

Only seconds had passed. There had been no struggle, no sound, no blood, and no regrets. Her death had not perturbed Karl in the slightest and, as the hall clock struck the hour, his sole concern was that his anger had caused him to be momentarily careless.

Killing the woman in broad daylight was risky, especially doing it so near the time when servants would be arriving at the manor. Lacking the cover of darkness to mask the murder, and anxious to avoid interaction with the help, Karl had been obliged to wrap Judith in a sheet and carry the bothersome woman to the garage. He placed her limp body on the rear seat of his Toyota Tacoma and covered it with a tarp.

By the time the housemaid arrived at nine o'clock, he'd already finished hitching up his boat trailer. He stood by his Tacoma and gave the woman a cursory wave. Then he left the manor, drove his rig to the Delta City hardware store, and paid cash for sixteen feet of chain and two padlocks.

When he emerged from the store, there was a problem in the parking lot. An undernourished boy was grappling with a leash and wrestling with an oversized dog while the animal lunged at the Toyota and barked incessantly.

Could this be a spontaneous connection between canine and cadaver? Karl asked himself.

"Do you have a saddle to ride that animal?" he asked aloud as he unloaded his purchases, attempting to strike a casual manner while using the shopping cart as a shield. The kid emitted an embarrassed laugh as the dog stopped barking, fixed its gaze on Karl, and produced a deep rumbling growl. Karl froze in his tracks and automatically reached for his pistol, momentarily forgetting that the weapon was locked in the Tacoma. "You had better hold that beast while I get in," he tried to project a demanding tone but failed to mask the apprehension in his voice.

The boy nodded, reeled in the leash, and attempted to restrain the aggressive animal. Karl was typically fearless, but dogs in general made him anxious and he harbored a particular dread of large dogs. It was an inconvenient anxiety which evoked a vivid trauma from Karl's past which leapt, unbidden, into his subconscious.

Decades ago, as a guard at a Nazi concentration camp, Karl had come to the attention of Dr. Wilhelm von Bismark who had the young corporal assigned to his laboratory. The doctor was strict, but Karl willingly submitted to a series of experiments which reduced the tedium of his military assignment and also granted him access to an ever-expanding array of camp privileges. Soon Karl was relieved of other duties and, when not in surgery, he was given the run of the camp, and he made the most of his new-found leisure. He soon became a fixture in the camp. An enigmatic and idle young man who seemed to have no purpose, he became known as Rumpelstiltskin—a satirical nickname used by guards and prisoners alike. The laboratory shared a courtyard with a training facility for military working dogs and the young corporal once made the mistake of interrupting a canine exercise. The trainers spotted him and shouted, Fass! Heeding the command to attack, unrestrained dogs gave chase and Karl was forced to retreat with a trio of powerful canines nipping at his heels. The dogs cornered him and crept ever nearer—snarling and barking—while the trainers took their sweet time before calling them off. It was a terrifying encounter which left an indelible impression on his younger self.

As that vision from his past had faded, Karl had started his Tacoma and left the boy, the meddlesome dog, and the city behind. Moments later, he was barreling along a narrow pavement, winding through a landscape of undulating dirt-brown hills which locals called the 'dobies. After a mile, he slowed down—it wouldn't do to invite a speeding ticket. When he reached Highway 65, he steered onto the broader pavement, turned northward, and negotiated a series of switchbacks leading to Grand Mesa. Halfway up, he pulled off the main highway and onto an isolated dirt lane. He followed the unimproved track for a quarter of a mile until he reached a thick stand of scrub oaks. Screened by the dense trees, he shut off the engine, exited the Toyota, scanned his surroundings, and listened.

Convinced he was alone, he opened the rear door, pulled the tarp aside, secured several chain lengths around Judith's winding sheet, and double-locked the chain ends together. Returning to the highway, he drove upward through the forest until he reached a narrow dirt road which led to the Island Lake marina. As he expected at the height of the summer tourist season, the marina parking area was nearly full, but all the vehicles were unoccupied—everyone was already out on the lake and fishing.

He backed down the boat ramp, unloaded his rowboat, tethered it to the primitive dock, then parked the Toyota. After making certain he was unobserved, he fitted the tarp around his former lover and carried her petite body to the boat. He added his fishing gear, locked up the Tacoma, then launched the craft and rowed to the middle of the 180-acre lake.

Island Lake was said to be the largest and deepest of the Mesa's three hundred lakes. That suited Karl fine—the broader and deeper the better. He shipped his oars and dropped anchor. The anchor took hold at fifty feet. He played out another twenty-feet of rope just in case the wind came up. Then he extracted his fly-rod from its protective case and proceeded to fish the August afternoon away. A dozen boaters passed by but, consistent with an unspoken fisherman's protocol, they kept their distance. Even so, Karl kept his head down, relying on the brim of his broad hat to obscure his features.

Hours later, the sun was slanting westward as other anglers abandoned the lake, loaded their boats, and drove home or returned to their camps. A paragon of patience, the calculating corporal waited until the marina parking lot was empty and until he could see fires being kindled in the lakeside campgrounds. As the long summer day faded, he remained on the water. At twilight, when he was certain he was alone, he removed the tarp, balanced Judith's chained body between the oar locks, and slid her over the side.

Her tiny corpse barely rippled the surface and the body sunk like a proverbial stone. For a fleeting second, Karl regretted not securing a trophy of his kill. She'd been wearing several items of jewelry—a broach, a necklace, a ring—all expensive gifts from himself. Any one of these would have served as a souvenir. Then he dismissed the thought. Back at the manor, the entire upstairs closet was brimming with relics in the form of dresses and shoes. What better tokens to memorialize his spendthrift lover?

At dusk, the unrepentant corporal had been rowing back to the marina when he glanced over his shoulder and saw someone standing on shore. The man was staring intently in Karl's direction, so intently that Karl looked back along the slip trail he'd left in the water and toward the far shore—thinking there must be something over there which was attracting the man's attention. But there was nothing to be seen. Obviously, the man was staring at him.

And for how long? he asked himself.

Karl guided the boat into the shallows and the man obligingly grabbed the prow to steady the vessel as Karl hopped out. The man stared at him with an expectant expression, so Karl decided to play the role of a foreign tourist.

"Guten Abend," Karl said in German. If the man understood him saying *good evening,* he didn't acknowledge the greeting.

"Kann ich ihnen helfen?" Karl asked aloud. Then silently, to himself, he translated his question: *Can I help you?* And, in his mind, he added, *Must I kill you?*

To his surprise, the man rattled off some nonsense in halting German—something about how to properly time a pork roast, if Karl understood him correctly. For a moment the two stared at one another, a pair of alpine statues, immobile in the dim light which steadily darkened the mountain shore. The stranger was dressed in rustic clothes topped by a ridiculous woolen cap with its oversized tassel drooping to one side. It was as if the old man had materialized from the past, an impression reinforced by the ancient fishing rod he held in one hand—a cane pole minus a reel. Given his odd speech and his vintage outfit, Karl decided the man was ninety if he was a day and obviously an idiot.

"Guten Abend," Karl repeated as he tied up his rowboat and walked away. He would deal with the boat eventually. For the time being, he'd return to his Tacoma.

Karl interrupted his recollection of last summer and this odd incident at Island Lake to pour himself a third drink. Only much later did the corporal learn that this chance encounter on the shore of Island Lake would mark his first encounter with Herbert Schulz, Grand Mesa's notorious hermit, and his future target. As it happened, the unexpected meeting was out of sequence. Karl hadn't yet been ordered to locate and kill the older man. The two men had interacted purely by chance—a happenstance which the fatalistic Karl, who didn't believe in coincidences, would ultimately attribute to his vision of a grand design.

At the time, Herbert Schulz was also blissfully unaware of any connection. The old man had been fishing from the bank all afternoon without success. He'd glimpsed Karl's boat anchored off-shore and he found it unusual that the craft remained in the same spot for hours. Either the stationary boater was catching fish out there, or he was killing time. Being curious, the old man had lingered at the marina because he hoped to learn what had kept someone out so late in a single portion of the lake on a day when the fish weren't biting. He hadn't seen Karl disposing of the body and he did not perceive the man, who was apparently a foreigner, as a threat. Herbert's only goal had been to ask about fishing, not realizing the man was apparently a tourist with limited English.

On that August evening, Karl had walked toward the Toyota. Moving casually but purposefully, he'd admired the subtle nature of his vehicle's muted exterior which made the Tacoma practically anonymous in the daytime and essentially invisible in the fading light. Karl had repainted it himself, spraying on a thick coating of automotive primer paint. He much preferred the Toyota's dull-gray finish to the sleek black sheen which lay beneath the muted primer. A glossy finish, in his opinion, made for a lustrous black car which had a tendency to reflect artificial and celestial lights. In his line of work, it didn't pay to be conspicuous.

The Tacoma was the only vehicle in the otherwise empty parking lot. But, given the truck's neutral color, the old man he'd left behind at the boat ramp might not have noticed Karl's Toyota. And, as for the elderly man himself and his faulty German, probably the old fool had no idea where he was or what he was saying. Perhaps the man had seen nothing or maybe he'd not seen enough to comprehend what Karl was up to.

Probably, perhaps, maybe, the cautious corporal thought. *But why take chances?*

As Karl approached the Tacoma, he considered the vehicle's inventory. His Walther P.38 was in the Tacoma's lockbox but climbing up into the bed to get the pistol might spook the man. Not only that but firing the noisy semi-automatic in this pristine alpine environment would attract immediate attention. The road leading up from the marina was narrow and it would only take one or two curiosity seekers in their wide-bodied vehicles to block his escape.

His knife in the glove box would be a handier weapon, a silent option, and easier to obtain without arousing suspicion. So, as Karl walked, he formulated a plan. He would unlock the truck's passenger-side door, smoothly open the glove box, and secretly slip the knife into his pocket. Then he'd walk around to the driver's seat, back the trailer up, and load the rowboat, enlisting the stranger to lend a hand. Once the man relaxed his guard, Karl would thrust the blade into his kidneys. Satisfied with his preparations to murder this potentially troublesome witness, the corporal turned back, expecting to give his intended victim a reassuring wave, but the old man had vanished.

Chapter 9

All-Nighter
(December 30 / Late)

Unwilling to disturb his slumbering wife, Trinidad Sands parked his Ridgeline near the corral, quietly opened and re-latched the truck door, and walked the rest of the way to the Lavender Hill farmhouse. Once inside, the detective tiptoed upstairs, slipped into the bedroom closet, and quietly obtained the bulky dry-bag containing Herbert Schulz's unpublished manuscript. Clutching the bag to his chest, he retraced his steps and was just easing the bedroom door closed when Annie awoke.

"You're about as subtle as a gorilla in a china shop," she suggested.

"Don't you mean bull, Dear?" he whispered.

"Bull is right," Annie agreed as she sat up in bed. "What time is it and just where do you think you're going?"

"It's late—or rather it's early—and I've got some reading to catch up on," Trinidad whispered.

"No need to whisper, Love," Annie smiled. "It's just the two of us."

"I'm whispering because I don't want to wake my darling wife," he said.

"Oh," she laughed, "that's a noble thought. I'll be sure to tell her when she wakes up."

"Good night," Trinidad crooned. "Sweet dreams."

"Hmm," she scoffed. "Don't let the door hit you in the butt on the way out," she suggested.

Arriving downstairs, Trinidad centered the dry-bag on the kitchen table. Then he filled the old coffeepot with water, shoveled grounds into the basket, plopped the pot on the stove, and turned on the burner. While the water circulated, he unzipped the bag, and extracted a wooden box. After unlatching the lid, he paused, and—just as he'd done months ago when he'd first opened the box—he whistled in astonishment. The box contained a ream of paper, every page neatly typewritten with uniform margins. Each double-spaced, typewritten line was a thing of beauty: flawless, symmetrical, and exact. Trinidad knew Herbert had been a perfectionist.

Thinking back, Trinidad recalled one of his frequent visits to the older man's isolated Grand Mesa cabin. While sipping coffee in Herbert's cozy living room, Trinidad had glimpsed Herbert's vintage Underwood manual typewriter —the only such machine which the detective had ever seen outside of a museum.

"Does that thing work?" Trinidad recalled asking his host.

"It just sits there," Herbert replied. "I'm the one who does all the work."

The aroma of percolated coffee pulled Trinidad back to the present. He poured himself a cup and began his task. No matter how long it took, he was determined to read the entire manuscript. Reading it would honor the memory of Herbert Schulz and parts of it might help the detective understand, perhaps even solve, the old man's murder.

As the chimes of the grandfather clock in the farmhouse hallway marked the passage of time, Trinidad worked his way through the first hundred pages. Some of it he already knew from conversations with Herbert: his early years growing up in Leadville as the son of a coal miner and then a miner himself until 1941 when he and a friend enlisted in the army. Eight weeks later, he found himself stationed in Hawaii at Schofield Barracks where he stood on the roof of his billet in his underwear, desperately firing his rifle at Japanese aircraft as they strafed and bombed the surrounding airfield and harbor.

Transferred to the European Theatre of Operations in 1944, he spent several months training in England where he sustained a leg wound by tripping over rural farm machinery in the dark. The wound became infected, and he developed impetigo, a contagious bacterial infection which is more common in children.

"My face and hands broke-out in the most appalling red boils," Herbert wrote. "I felt like a teenager again with all the problems of pimples which plague that age. Worst of all, I was confined to quarters and unable to be with the other lads. That was the worst of it."

The infection cleared up in time for him to join the landing forces on D-Day 1944. He was wounded on the beach and nearly suffocated beneath a mound of bodies as scores of his ambushed comrades fell on top of him. Eventually he was assigned to a scouting squad which meant he was sent out in the dark to discover enemy positions and strength. On one such mission, everyone else in his squad was killed, and he was captured. He spent time in a prisoner of war camp but was subsequently rescued by advancing Canadians and reassigned to provide infantry support to a tank battalion.

"Our tank duty was a step-up from the hazards of night patrols," Herbert wrote. "But you had to watch yourself at all times since those tank-jockeys drove their machines like they were hotrods. You wouldn't believe the way they spun those monster treads around. And the noise! It's impossible to describe the chaos of those mechanical monsters exchanging fire with the enemy. In the heat of battle, the turmoil was nerve-shattering—tanks rumbling, turrets whirling,

76-millimeter cannons thundering, machine-guns pulsing. Hell on Earth it was."

As his unit pushed into Germany in the closing months of the war, he found himself in a destroyed town where he rescued his future wife. Trinidad was familiar with that encounter, and it paralleled the spoken tale which Herbert had related to him and which the detective, in turn, shared with Annie.

"Such a love," Annie had said and no sooner had Trinidad recalled her words than he heard the sound of his wife padding downstairs in her stocking feet. Entering the kitchen, she kissed the top of his head, and set about fixing breakfast.

"One egg or two?" she asked.

"Two and bacon please," he requested. "I just finished reading the *such a love* part of Herbert's autobiography—you'll recall how he pulled Meeska out of a bombed-out basement."

"How could I forget?" she asked. "A sure-fire Hallmark Channel, made-for-TV movie, in my humble opinion."

"Hmm," said Trinidad as he fished a fresh page out of its wooden box.

"Good hum, or bad hum?" Annie asked.

"Puzzled hum," her husband responded as he shifted through a few more pages. "I could be wrong, but I think there's a page missing. No—here it is. Somehow, they got out of order. Good thing the pages are numbered. That's a relief because this meandering tale is just about to wander into—for me at least—uncharted territory. This appears to be Meeska's backstory and background tales concerning Father Thomas and Caroline Liberstein—stories Herbert never shared with me. Maybe things he never shared with anyone."

"Except for Jack who we know has a copy of a portion of the manuscript," Annie suggested. "And probably Caroline, don't you imagine?"

"Pillow talk?" Trinidad surmised.

"Exactly," Annie smiled.

While Annie rustled up breakfast, Trinidad was transported into the past by the manuscript's vivid description of Meeska's experiences as a youthful civilian in Nazi Germany. In fact, the writing was a bit too detailed, and the detective suspected that Meeska herself had authored this section. He pictured her writing her part by hand and imagined the bittersweet process Herb had undertaken to transcribe his late wife's handwritten pages. Her command of English was as impeccable as her German and—according to Herbert—she had also mastered French. She grew up as the privileged daughter of a wealthy Berlin merchant who seemingly cooperated with the Fascist government while secretly channeling weapons and munitions to the French Resistance. When her father's duplicity was discovered, her parents were both imprisoned. She and her older sister lived for a time with a Berlin uncle then fled the city to live with her mother's younger brother, who owned a Remagen bakery.

When word came that her parents had been executed, Meeska—who was then a girl of twelve—vowed to revenge their deaths. She and her older sister joined a homegrown White Rose resistance group and channeled their anger and grief into the risky business of distributing anti-fascist leaflets. They also sabotaged Nazi transportation by pouring sugar into the gas tanks of unguarded vehicles in order to clog fuel filters. Then, when sugar became too dear to sacrifice, the girls used bleach and plain water.

But their most ingenious disruption ingredient came in the form of a wartime soda pop—a fabricated Nazi substitute for Coca-Cola. Prior to World War II, there were nearly four-dozen Coke plants in Germany. But during the war, America cut off the supply of the secret formula needed to manufacture the popular drink. Casting about for a substitute, local chemists came up with something resembling diluted ginger ale which was dubbed Fanta—an abbreviated version of the German word for *fantastic* or *fantasy*. The Third Reich's Fanta concoction was a mulligan stew of waste products generated by other food industries—dregs left over from cider production, discarded whey gleaned from the making of cheese, a weak concentration of sugar coaxed from beets, and anything else which inventors could afford on a wartime budget.

"I never cared for Coca-Cola," the writer—presumably Meeska—proclaimed. "And I liked this new bastardized beverage even less. Therefore, it was no great sacrifice to upturn bottle after bottle into the vulnerable gas tanks of the vehicles of war."

Meanwhile, aircraft were continually bombarding troop concentrations and industrial centers. The author was never certain whether Allied or Nazi bombs leveled the Remagen bakery, but the family was living in the flat above the business and, in a fury of pre-dawn noise and confusion an entire urban block was destroyed. Meeska's uncle was away on business, but she was trapped in the rubble and her sister was killed there. As if to verify Trinidad's suspicion that Meeska had authored much of the middle portions of the manuscript, what happened next had been written in the first person.

"I lay in darkness, unable to move, barely able to breathe, and incapable of crying out. Later, I felt, rather than saw, the sun rising. Whereupon, I gathered my courage and shouted for help. I heard scrabbling and prepared to face whatever rescuer God had seen fit to provide me, be that person angel or devil. God be thanked, it was the former."

The next several pages confirmed Trinidad's recollection of the story which Herbert Schulz had shared with the detective during one of their many Pancake House conversations. The rescue, the parting, the exchange of passionate correspondence, the reunion, and a shared life of love. New details also emerged. In particular, the detective learned the story of Meeska's unique dowry and how that wedding bequest intertwined the lives of four wartime survivors who came to inhabit the wild Western Slope of Colorado within a stone's throw of one another.

"Take a break?" Annie asked.

"Love to," said Trinidad as he accepted a heaping plateful of scrambled eggs, toast, and bacon. "You know," he added between bites, "I hope, when our story is written, that it will be even half as memorable as this typewritten saga is turning out to be."

"Only half?" Annie frowned. "I'd better get busy thinking up more drama and snappier adventures—otherwise our future audience will walk out during the first act."

"I'm certain you'll hold their attention, Dear, even when they tire of me," he assured her.

"The B.S. is getting pretty deep in here," she chided. "Should I go get my boots on?"

"Point taken," he laughed. "Anyway, you should read this. It's pretty good. Plus, I now have a line on something called the *war nickels.*"

"Nickel as in a coin?" Annie asked.

"Correct, but I'm talking nickels with an 's' and not just a handful or a dozen. Apparently, when Meeska made her way by ship to post-war America in 1946, the blushing bride was accompanied by an entire barrelful of the gleaming silvery coins."

"That had to weigh a ton, yes?"

"A couple of tons probably," Trinidad guessed. "A barrel

could be as large as 50-plus gallons and could hold as many as 487,600 nickels and—"

"Cheater—you're reading that off your smartphone!" Annie grumbled.

"I'm merely reciting the answer to a text message which I sent earlier to our resident coin expert," Trinidad confirmed.

"You texted Dallas Heckleson?" Annie said. "For shame, waking the old ranger up like that."

"Just like me, he was awake all night," said Trinidad.

"Insomnia?"

"Depression," Trinidad said. "Turns out our old friend has a case of the winter blues, and a math problem involving collectible coins was a welcome distraction. The numbers haven't stopped rolling in since around midnight."

Trinidad was having such a good time reporting his results that Annie hadn't the heart to tell her earnest husband that her graduate schoolwork at The University of Arizona had already supplied her with a more than adequate knowledge of the war nickel phenomenon.

Annie knew that, during World War II, when key metals were needed to manufacture armor plating, nickel was a rationed commodity, and the U.S. Mint was ordered to stop using it. As a result, substitute American five-cent pieces which were minted from 1942 to 1945 contained absolutely no nickel. Instead, thousands of so-called war nickels were minted using an alloy of copper, silver, and manganese.

Much trial and error was needed to get the weight correct so that the newly-conceived coins would function in vending machines and pay telephones.

Eventually, the modified coins were redesigned to contain 56% copper, 35% silver, and 9% manganese. Working with her late university professor, Annie had witnessed a classroom experiment which analyzed the contents of the wartime coins.

Thinking of Dr. Clark and his tragic end, Annie involuntarily sniffed. If her professor hadn't dispatched her on a university geocaching trip, she'd never have taken the road to Lavender, never have been put in harm's way, never lost Professor Clark, and never met and married Trinidad.

These bittersweet memories flashed through her subconscious, and she was tempted to interject them into the conversation. Instead, she decided to defer to her spouse and resist playing the expert.

"So, our Texas Ranger Emeritus knows all about these so-called *war nickels*?" she asked.

"Yup," Trinidad answered. "If they're genuine war nickels, he estimates each coin is 35% silver, weighs about 5 grams, and is worth at least $25."

"I don't suppose he figured out the value of all the coins in this hypothetical barrel," she wondered.

"Something over half a million dollars if melted down," Trinidad reported. "Maybe twice to three times that amount if individual coins are sold to collectors and four times that amount for the odd coin which has a defect or two."

"A defect like a moustache on Thomas Jefferson?" she joked.

"More like missing symbols, or letters overlapping the coin rim, or cracks in the President's forehead caused by the errant strike of a minting machine or faulty die casting—stuff like that," Trinidad added after consulting a string of text messages.

"That old ranger needs a hobby," she said.

"He already has one, apparently," said Trinidad. "If coin collecting counts."

"Well," Annie chided, "can you tear yourself away from your phone for ten seconds and tell me what the Schulz manuscript says became of that hefty nickel barrel?"

"That's a bit unclear so far," Trinidad admitted. "As near as I can figure from the manuscript, when his wife died, Herbert and the others decided to bury both Meeska *and* the barrel."

"Bury—as in a grave?"

"It might simply mean that Meeska's death compelled others to hide the barrel somewhere. Apparently, it was a source a friction between the surviving parties," he said.

"Survivors meaning Herbert Schulz, Father Thomas, and Caroline," she surmised.

"Seems so," Trinidad mused. "I'll know more when I take up the narrative. Or do you want to read it yourself?"

"Tell you what, cowboy," Annie said. "After you help me with the breakfast dishes, if you're up for it, how about I curl up on the living room sofa and you read aloud to me—like a radio program—that'd be a treat."

"I believe I can stay awake to do that," Trinidad yawned. "Although I'm gonna need more coffee to pull it off."

"Done and done," Annie laughed. "You do the dishes and I'll start a fresh pot."

After breakfast, the couple adjourned to the living room where Annie took over the sofa and made a nest of blankets for herself while Trinidad settled into the rocking chair.

"Are you certain-sure you can balance that wonky box on your lap?" she asked. "I'd hate to see you spill all those carefully-ordered pages."

"I've been rocking since I was five," he assured his wife. "There was a time I could roll a cigarette and knit a sweater while riding a horse."

"Hmm. My diagnosis is I think you're getting a bit punchy from staying up too late," she said, her tone reflecting genuine concern. "How about we call a time-out, and you take a nap, and we reconvene in a couple of hours then—"

She didn't finish the thought because, with a box on his lap and a single manuscript sheet in one hand, her weary husband had ceased rocking and fallen fast asleep. Annie stood up and gently relieved her drowsy husband of his box and paper. Then, after placing the boxed manuscript carefully on the living room floor, she led Trinidad to the sofa and tucked a blanket under his chin.

"Good night, Sweet Prince," she said. "And flights of angels sing thee to thy rest."

"Shakespeare," Trinidad mumbled.

"Bingo," Annie confirmed as she took a seat on the floor, leaned against the sofa, and reached into the manuscript box. "Now, let's see what comes next," she whispered.

Chapter 10

Trophy

(December 31 / 2:00 a.m.)

The manor's hall clock struck twice, and Corporal Karl Bistro checked his watch. He'd wasted too much time revisiting old memories. He was sentimental, after a fashion. It was a trait he preferred to suppress. The past was gone. He needed to focus on the present and, of course, there was the future to consider.

Time goes only forward, he reminded himself. *No one can undo the past, which serves only as a cautionary tale—nothing more. Indulging the past is futile, you must return your thoughts to the present.*

Always before, after a kill, his intractable habit had been to swallow a sedative and enjoy a long and untroubled nap. It was part of his ritual and also essential to preserve his health. He shouldn't have taken so much alcohol. The sedative, and therefore his refreshing nap, would have to wait.

Standing at the manor's well-stocked bar, the corporal studied his reflection in an undamaged section of the mirror. Observers would be hard-pressed to guess his age. For that miracle, Karl had to thank Dr. Wilhelm von Bismark and his magical *Alternative-Lengthening-of-Telomeres* mechanism.

Karl didn't pretend to understand the science of A.L.T. There was no need. All Karl knew or cared to know about A.L.T. was the fact that he himself was a living, breathing example of the procedure's success. Von Bismark was a brilliant surgeon and patriot whose party loyalty was beyond question and the old doctor had done all he could to advance the Third Reich. Young Karl was a soldier in Nazi Germany and, as such, his duty had been clear.

In those days, the trusting corporal put himself, literally, into Dr. von Bismark's hands. The persistent surgeries and perpetual inoculations had been relentless and painful, but Karl couldn't argue with the results. He'd been twenty-three in 1940 when von Bismark went to work on him. Since that time, he hadn't aged a day. His age was the same and so was his unwavering resolve to remain a loyal servant of his Nazi masters.

Neo-Nazis, someone had called them, but Karl preferred to drop the *Neo-* prefix. There was nothing new about Karl's loyalty to the cause. The old dreams were still best and the greatest potential for realizing those classic visions rested with an immortal such as himself. The need for sleep and proper diet were essential for Karl—they were the indominable keys to maintaining the elongated life which had been granted him. These were small prices to pay for the chance to live forever.

Karl smiled and reminded himself how utterly impossible it would have been to logically explain his existence to any of the countless and exceedingly ordinary human beings he'd encountered during his artificially extended lifetime. With Judith, he'd been tempted to indulge in such an explanation and that indiscretion had resulted in betrayal.

Best to accept the inescapable fact that no mere mortal can possibly understand what you are, he told himself. *Best to accept that truth and move on.*

Abandoning the manor bar, the dedicated corporal sought out his pen and journal. To make best use of the time, he'd write out his account of yesterday's murder. Then he would eat. Then he would sleep. He walked forty-nine steps to his vintage roll-top desk, switched on the nearby lamp, and took a seat.

In his flowing hand, he wrote his summary of his latest kill.

I dispatched the target, Herbert Schulz, at daybreak, gathered up my trophy, and lingered in the shadows of the crime scene—savoring the thrill of rubbing elbows with local authorities who were tasked with solving the murder. After workers had carved a staging area in the deep snow, I waited as officials began to populate that area, and inserted myself into the scene. I observed the comings and goings of officials and lay volunteers. I engaged a select few in conversation, drank their coffee, and sampled their saccharine pastries. Not a single person acknowledged my improvised presence. Nor did anyone challenge me or ask me to account for myself.

I spent the entire day in the snow on Grand Mesa, until well-past dark. Then I slipped away, drove back to the manor, attended to my rifle, and briefly compromised my otherwise disciplined life by drinking alcohol and reminiscing about the past.

The corporal wrote candidly and was unsparing in his self-critique. He denounced his impulsive actions and yet—even as he wrote—he couldn't resist the urge to indulge his memories. Perhaps, if he wrote down everything which occurred to him, he could better comprehend and thereby purge from his life these wasteful inefficiencies. Karl paused in his writing, smiled, and glanced across his trophy room in the direction of the broad fireplace. The old man's ridiculous cap was there on the mantle, draped over the handle of a silver loving cup. The cup was an oversized prize he'd won decades ago as crew captain of a sailing team, sweeping all honors at a highly competitive San Diego regatta.

Retaining and displaying the sailing cup had been a reasonable act—an understandable sign of vanity. On the other hand, his decision to keep Schulz's colorful headgear had been irrational. Preserving evidence was foolish and hazardous. From his brushes with the judicial system, Karl knew that there are different types of evidence. *Demonstrative evidence* represents or verifies a crime—photographs or video or audio recordings are classic examples. *Testimonial evidence* includes eyewitness accounts of what was seen or heard at the crime scene. *Documentary evidence* constitutes a paper trail encompassing such items as deeds, contracts, correspondence, and other tangible documents. Such evidence can either be *exculpatory* (proving one's innocence) or *inculpatory* (confirming one's guilt.)

Any detective or prosecutor worth his salt would be satisfied to go to trial with demonstrative, testimonial, and documentary evidence in hand. However, when seeking a conviction, nothing trumps real evidence in the form of tangible objects which have been present at or utilized at the scene of the crime. Classic examples are murder weapons, footprints, fingerprints, and blood-soaked apparel. Scattered among the stitches and seams of the old man's wool cap were sufficient splotches of freshly spattered blood to make the purloined item a bonanza of compelling evidence which was both *real* and particularly *inculpatory*.

Striving to remain honest and objective in his written self-assessment, Karl had to admit that keeping the cap was foolhardy. But doing so was also irresistible, because it had proven impossible to break his lifelong habit of retaining a souvenir from each of his kills. Over the years, he'd accumulated a host of innocuous items—thirty-two to be exact—stretching back to the first trophy he'd acquired on the mean streets of East Berlin.

It was odd that the corporal—though trained as a sniper, then recruited as a prison guard—had survived the Second World War without killing anyone—without even firing a shot in anger. He never saw combat. Beginning in 1940, and ending with von Bismark's suicide in 1945, the doctor's pervasive procedures had monopolized the young soldier's every waking hour. Even his infrequent periods of sleep were monitored and manipulated. For all intents and purposes, young Karl spent five years in a laboratory world which—with the single exception of his frightening encounter with a trio of snarling dogs—was insulated from chaos. Throughout those turbulent years, as the war swirled around him, he'd remained apart, enclosed in an experimental cocoon of oblivion.

Eventually, World War II ended, followed by recriminations, trials, and a measure of reconciliation. History books suggest that the end of the war meant that Fascism was defeated and eradicated. Karl knew better. Certain ideas are hard to kill. He was living evidence of this inescapable fact. No one remembered the First Reich or Second and the Third Reich had become a steadily fading memory. The Fourth Reich—the realm which Karl and others would bring to fruition—was just around the corner and no one would see that glorious day coming until it was too late.

Chapter 11

First Kill
(December 31 / 2:15 a.m.)

The manor's hall clock struck a quarter-hour. Despite the time, Corporal Karl Bistro remained awake as he rekindled the memory of his first kill. The corporal was a product of the Second World War, but it was not until 1989 that he was assigned by his master to take a life. Karl had never met his master in person—he merely presumed, since all his superiors during the war had been males, that his master was a man. Absent any specific knowledge, Karl visualized his anonymous master to be a rotund, white-haired gentleman with a flowing beard. Not unlike an idealized vision of Santa Claus. His instructions came in the form of letters or telegrams, and later as cellphone texts, everything written in code with no return address. The corporal never asked about anything, and he never questioned his orders.

His first victim had been an anonymous East Berlin prostitute—an expendable target who, in accordance with general characteristics which were dictated by his master, was selected for him by an infamous Russian mob known as the Scarlet Brotherhood. It was a test of loyalty which the mob required of all their recruits, especially those who had once served the Nazi cause.

His initial kill was to be a cold-blooded murder at close range, quite unlike his sniper training. There was no uniformed enemy, no homeland to defend, no political agenda, no cause involved. It was a rite of passage, the cost of doing business, a simple yet necessary task, which Karl undertook without hesitation. The woman was unlikely to be missed—an unnamed streetwalker, apparently selected at random by the Brotherhood. He'd accosted his assigned victim at dawn on an abandoned street corner, intending to cut her throat, but she'd evaded his grasp, and he ended up chasing her. In the end, she broke through a flimsy railing and fell to her death without uttering a sound.

Odd that she didn't cry out, he remembered thinking then and he had the same thought each time he recalled that significant morning in his mind. *What sort of woman would have gone to her death so silently—so willingly?* Or was he over-thinking it? Possibly she had merely been surprised by the crumbling railing and unable to comprehend that her fatal fall would be her last Earthly act.

On that long-ago morning, young Karl had arrived at the railing just as the woman went over. Instinctively, he'd reached for his victim but only managed to tangle his fingers in the delicate chain encircling her neck. The chain had broken free as she fell, leaving him holding the dead woman's pendant.

Karl still possessed that pendant—that token of his first kill.

He pressed his chest and felt the object dangling there on his own necklace which he wore beneath his shirt. For years he'd worn that crude bauble—a lump of metal with the initials H.E.A. scratched on it. He'd never known what the letters stood for. At first, he'd tried to deduce their meaning, conjuring up the most fantastic combinations, until at last he stopped guessing.

Accepting the letters as an impenetrable mystery, he reminded himself of his grandmother's sage advice. *Die Kirche im Dorf Lassen,* it was something the old woman said whenever his boyhood imagination ran amuck. "Leave the church in the village," she told her impetuous grandson—*in other words, my fanciful boy, do not get carried away.*

Lucky for him, whatever the bauble's hidden meaning, the Brotherhood had accepted the pendant as proof of death and counted the prostitute's demise as a legitimate kill—one which earned him an apprenticeship with the infamous cartel. Joining the Scarlet Brotherhood, Karl had quickly acquired a reputation as a dependable and bloodthirsty underling. He'd soon become a sought-after agent who asked no questions and did as he was told while also possessing sufficient cunning to improvise when necessary. Such attributes had allowed him to rise rapidly through the ranks, acquiring power and money as he advanced.

By the time his master ordered him to cut ties with the Russian mob and return to his Nazi roots, Karl had amassed not only a wealth of deadly experience, but a tidy nest-egg as well. Living off the interest from shrewd investments, he could have easily retired, but he was loyal to the Reich. Anyone who thought the Nazis had been vanquished in 1945 would be in for a rude awakening when Karl and his fellow supermen took their rightful places to claim dominion over the unwary World. The Master Race was very much alive, more devoted than ever, and destined to rise again.

Besides, even if his politics had not remained unchanged, the sadistic corporal was unwilling to abandon the thrill of the chase and the perverse pleasure he gleaned from looking his victims in the eyes in order to watch the light of life steadily extinguish. This obsessive desire for personal contact with his prey was intended to compensate for the opportunity which had eluded him during his first kill. Dissatisfied with losing his prostitute over the railing without a face-to-face encounter, he'd made it a point to be eye-to-eye with his succeeding targets.

He'd dispatched Judith at close range and—even though that murder had been personal—it had furthered his Nazi agenda. If Judith had turned informer, completing his Western Colorado assignment would have become much more difficult. Yesterday morning, of course, he'd been obliged to dispatch the troublesome Schulz from a distance. The instant he'd fired that fatal and faraway shot, the corporal had been miffed, recalling that the old man would have been well within reach, if only he'd had more timely access to his target.

Hours ago, when he'd taken the distant shot which ended the life of Herbert Schulz, the corporal had viewed it as an unfulfilling reminder of his first murder. Both kills represented exceptions to his preferred modus operandi. But now, as he recorded his actions in his journal, Karl found himself smiling at the symmetry encompassed by his very first victim, the unlucky prostitute, and his most recent target.

Years ago, he'd been unable to overtake and make eye contact with the nameless prostitute. And yesterday, he'd arrived too late to confront his latest victim at close quarters. Schulz had already abandoned the shoreline bench where he'd donned skates near the edge of the frozen lake. But Karl had his orders, the clock was ticking, and his target was already far out onto the ice. So, the well-trained sniper had pressed his rifle to his shoulder and taken aim.

It had been early, and the sun had not yet cleared the surrounding peaks. Despite the circumstances, Karl had considered the scene to be picturesque. The forest and the lake and the sky were all blending into a single shade of steadily-lightening crimson. Karl recalled thinking that a person could never get his eyes full of this amazing country. In the gathering dawn, Schulz's colorful cap had been clearly visible as he skated effortlessly away toward the center of the ice. The old man had become a moving target.

So, Karl had improvised and used a lakeside bench to steady his aim. He found that the stone bench—which occupied a sheltered spot beneath the boughs of an evergreen and was thus entirely free of snow—made an excellent gun-rest. Peering through his telescopic sight, he'd focused on Schulz's rhythmically bobbing cap, then lowered the crosshairs to the target's broad back, waited for the old man to glide and recover, and squeezed the trigger. A customized silencer had muffled the report of the rifle so that Karl heard only two muted sounds: an initial thump as the bullet left the muzzle and an instantaneous second thud as the bullet struck the unlucky skater.

While Schulz lay helpless on the frozen lake, Karl had fastened ice crampons to the bottoms of both boots and walked at a leisurely pace out onto the ice, cradling his rifle as he watched the old man for movement. When he reached the spot where Schulz's cap lay on the ice, the trophy-seeking corporal had bent down to retrieve the thing and stuff it into his coat pocket. Then, seeing the prone man weakly raise his head, the gifted assassin smoothly aimed and placed a second slug in Schulz's forehead.

Returning to the shore, Karl had sat down to remove his crampons which he placed in another coat pocket. Then he slung his rifle, left the old man's boots, snowshoes, and jacket where they lay on the bench, and started back up the snowmobile trail. The snow on the upward-leading path was hard-packed and frigid which allowed him to stay on top of the base and walk all the way to the top without leaving a traceable boot mark.

"How I love this Arctic weather," the corporal said aloud as he continued to traverse the rigid snow until he reached his Tacoma, climbed into the bed, carefully placed his rifle in its case, and locked the bed-box. He revved up the engine and headed for the highway, steering haphazardly, and spinning all four tires on purpose to defeat any chance of some crackerjack forensic technician obtaining a tire mold.

He'd driven two miles down Highway 65 before deciding to pull over and turn off his headlights. He parked in a handy alcove, isolated from the pavement, where a passing plow operator had previously deposited a solid wall of snow which towered over, and thus obscured, his vehicle. This was a prudent measure to make certain no vehicle was following. As he waited, he turned on the radio and tuned it to the weather station which predicted, for the coming day, fifteen mile-per-hour winds gusting up to twenty-five point nine.

Just enough wind, Karl supposed, to remove any lingering trace of his footprints or his vehicle tracks.

"Perfect," he'd said aloud as he guided the digital dial away from the artificial sing-song voice of the computerized weather report to select his favorite FM station.

The Paul Lucas Trio had filled the cab of his Tacoma with mellow jazz as Karl returned to the highway, steered through switchbacks, and zigzagged down the southern flanks of Grand Mesa. As he entered the final turn, he could see the rooftops of Lavender twinkling in the near distance. Beyond the small village, the bulk of Delta City smudged the middle ground. Farther away, the snow-clad peaks of the West Elks and the San Juan Mountains seemed to float along the far horizon, to the east and the south respectively, like frosted battleships. Karl reached up and slid the overhead panel back to expose the sunroof. There were no clouds in the slowly brightening sky above and it promised to be a clear winter day.

As sunlight and jazz washed over him, Karl had considered how long it might take for this morning's murder to be discovered. He'd purposely left the body where it fell, fully intending it to be found—trusting that the killing would keep the local authorities involved while he put the finishing touches on what his late lover had so crassly dubbed his "nickel fixation."

He had nearly reached his intersecting escape route when he had a delicious and devilish thought. Rather than proceeding to Brimstone Corner, then returning to Coal-Slide Canyon and the secure confines of his isolated manor, he made a broad U-turn and pointed the Tacoma back uphill.

Instead of fleeing the scene, he'd indulge a whim. He'd drive partway up, park once again behind the screening snow wall, and remain there until the body was discovered. Increased activity on the highway, more vehicles, lights and sirens, would suffice to alert him. Patiently biding his time, he'd wait while local authorities assembled at Island Lake. Then he'd return to the scene of the crime, slip into the picture as an anonymous interloper, and make a self-indulgent appearance under the very noses of his adversaries. It might take a while, but he had every confidence that things would soon be in motion. Like a row of teetering dominos, one factor was destined to tumble into another, and Karl fervently desired to experience, first-hand, every delicious aspect of the cascading chain reaction which was about to alarm and disorient Western Colorado.

Chapter 12

Fresh Kill

(December 31 / 3:00 a.m.)

In order to reconstruct a complete and accurate record of his activities, Corporal Karl Bistro decided to remain awake while reviewing additional background material which he had included in an earlier edition of his written report. A month prior to the murder of Herbert Schulz, Karl had learned the identity of his intended victim. Thus, the diligent corporal began shadowing the old man and keeping a record of his findings:

November 16, 2019: Ever since I spotted Schulz and his conspicuous cap at the Delta City Market, I have kept my target under close scrutiny. If it had not been for the old man's ridiculous cap, I would not have recollected our chance encounter at the Island Lake marina where Schulz may or may not have witnessed me disposing of Judith's body. My master's orders had placed me in Western Colorado and compelled me to dwell in the tiny Village of Lavender with instructions to locate and reclaim a stash of purloined war nickels, while also dispatching certain elderly individuals. The location of the nickels was unknown, and the descriptions of my targets were vague. During the war, one of my targets had been an Allied soldier and two of my targets had been prisoners in the same camp where I was fortunate enough to endure my medical procedures. But, unlike myself, the prisoners—one male and one female—had aged—although somewhat gradually. Their uncharacteristic vigor, despite advanced years, gives credence to my master's assumptions that these prisoners had also been subjected to wartime experimentation and had, probably unwittingly, been endowed with certain benefits where aging was concerned. Furthermore, these two former prisoners had adopted aliases. So, for those beyond Schulz himself, who had done nothing to obscure his identity, all I had were dated inmate photographs and the original names Wolfgang Kjolhede and Gerda Vogel—not much to go on. And yet, I have, over the years, made do with much less.

As it was, spotting the cap was enough to trigger my memory of Schulz's halting German. I also recalled my passing estimate of his chronological age and so I pursued what the Americans call a "hunch." This supposition was sufficient to confirm that the old fool at the Island Lake marina and Schulz were one and the same.

It is, at present, mid-November, not yet Thanksgiving Day, and still unseasonably warm in the village, although the snow on Grand Mesa is already deep and getting deeper. While keeping Schulz under surveillance this morning, I saw the old man sitting with a gaggle of male cronies—all gathered around three round tables pushed haphazardly together in the market's deli. The group consisted of men of a certain age sitting in plastic chairs and all fortified with black coffee as they took turns "shooting the breeze."

On that November day, when Schulz had finally left the coffee klatch, Karl had followed as the old man gassed up and ran errands. He'd kept Schulz's vintage jeep in sight until sundown and then he'd followed taillights as the old hermit drove up onto the Grand Mesa. It was a clear autumn evening, and the temperature was mild although Highway 65 was lined with mounds of freshly-plowed snow. Eventually, the jeep veered off the highway and onto a primitive road which, for all intents and purposes, might have doubled as a stream bed.

Quickly scanning the surrounding topography and estimating that the route ahead was destined to double back on itself in a sweeping curve as it ascended a steep hill, the pursuing corporal parked his Tacoma. Hurriedly donning snowshoes and night vision goggles, Karl worked his way cross-country until he found the upper reaches of the roadway. He took no weapon. This was a scouting mission.

Having reached his chosen vantage point, Karl had been crossing over the narrow road to find better cover when he'd heard Schulz's jeep laboring uphill. He just had time to scurry across the roadway and crouch down before the droning vehicle rounded a corner and trundled past. Karl remained hidden in a knot of screening brush and watched as the old man's jeep reached another corner then appeared to drive straight into the base of a dense stand of subalpine firs, whereupon the darkness seemed to swallow the vehicle's taillights. The jeep's noisy engine stopped abruptly and, in the deep silence which followed, Karl heard a car door slam, then all was quiet again. He waited a full fifteen minutes before carefully returning to the narrow roadway and walking slowly toward the spot where he'd seen the jeep disappear.

As he approached the place, the alert corporal donned his goggles and made his way forward using the green-tinged glow of enhanced night-vision. When he reached the spot, he discovered the old man's jeep wedged beneath the sheltering cover of a small carport. The sides of the primitive structure had been sandwiched between two stands of trees and its metal roof was completely covered with snow and interlacing branches. There had to be a cabin somewhere in the dense forest, but there was no obvious path leading away from the carport, and, despite his night-vision gear, Karl didn't relish the idea of thwacking through snowy trees in the dark to search for a dwelling.

Besides, there was no point in bearding the old man in his den just yet. Schulz most certainly had to die, but first Karl would follow the man a bit longer to get a feel for his routine and also gather more information. Once he knew for certain when the old man would be absent from his alpine lair, Karl would locate the cabin and search the place. Whether or not the search bore fruit, he was obligated to kill the old buzzard eventually. In any event, the killing would not take place in Schulz's isolated cabin because, whatever else happened, the point was for the body to be found and the sooner the better.

Karl had first followed the jeep on a Friday and on the following day he'd made discrete inquiries and had learned that the old man came to town on a predictable schedule and wasn't due back again for another two weeks. The inquisitive corporal also caught wind of a rumor that Schulz may know something about a hidden cache of coins, and he intercepted gossip that the old man kept a journal in which he recorded past and current events. The coincidental encounter at the Island Lake marina was one thing—references to writing and persistent talk about coins represented a call to action. Karl's mandatory search for the missing nickels had drawn a blank. The rumors surrounding the old man, if true, would constitute a major breakthrough.

On Sunday afternoon, Karl had returned to Grand Mesa where he discovered an abandoned bow-hunter's platform which offered a view of the area beyond the old man's hidden carport. With binoculars around his neck, water bottles and groceries in his daypack, and a heavy-duty sleeping bag tucked under one arm, Karl climbed into the nest. Regardless of this elevated viewpoint, he was unable to spot the cabin, but he was determined to wait in the growing cold.

He spent the night there and on Monday morning, he noticed smoke rising from the old man's chimney—an observation which allowed him to pinpoint the cabin's location. Watching until Schulz departed, Karl climbed down and conducted a thorough search of the isolated structure. He discovered no coins and no journal—nothing except a trunkful of old love letters which, in his anger, Karl had been tempted to hurl into the stove. But it was too soon to alert Schulz that he was being watched. Besides, burning the letters would have undone the elaborate precautions the efficient assassin had taken to traverse the snow surrounding the remote cabin while leaving no trace of his passage. Returning to his observation platform to gather his things, Karl abandoned that post but found other opportunities to continue his surveillance, keeping detailed records of the old man's activities.

After compiling observations for two solid weeks, Karl wrote for instructions, and waited. At last, a message arrived, and the contents set Monday, December 30, as the date of Schulz's demise. The choice of days seemed prophetic. Schulz needed to die, and Karl knew exactly where the old man would be every Monday morning. Given the old man's routine, it would be most practical to kill him at Island Lake.

Before dawn, Karl drove up toward the frozen lake, intent on ambushing Schulz on the shoreline. But a carload of tourists had stopped to pose for winter photos on the bluff at the intersection of Highway 65 and the snowy road which circled around the broad lake. So, Karl had been obliged to drive on by, park further up the highway, and wait for the visitors to leave. As a result of this unexpected delay, he'd come too late to surprise the old man on the shore and yet he'd managed to shoot Schulz on the ice.

Improvisation, he'd told himself.

When the deed was finally done, Karl had started for home only to change his mind. If the corporal had continued on, he'd be well clear of the crime scene before anyone spotted the body. Impetuously, he'd decided to savor the thrill of returning to the scene of the crime.

Closing his journal, Karl climbed the stairs to his second-story bedroom. Before retiring, he'd indulge in his habitual ritual of playing a simulated game of draw poker. As was his customary practice, he sat at a round wooden table and dealt four hands of five cards each—distributing cards face-up to three imaginary opponents and face-down to himself. Then, acting as dealer, he improved each face-up hand in turn by discarding and drawing an appropriate number of cards. Only then did he look at his own hand and attempt to better it.

The ritual was an exercise in integrity (sincerely trying to enhance the cards of his imagined adversaries) and chance (testing the margins of Fate.) Surprisingly, he often won, even when one of his pseudo foes managed to assemble a presumably unassailable hand. He once defeated an ace-to-ten of hearts by drawing to a spade royal flush. On such occasions, he reminded his phantom opposition of the traditional ranking of suits. Rather than relying on the idea that the suits are ranked in descending alphabetical order: spades to hearts to diamonds to clubs, he had invented his own rubric:

"Death (represented by the gravedigger's *spade*) is the most powerful. Love (naturally represented by the *heart*) is reduced to second rank. Wealth (*diamond*) takes third position. And War (symbolized by the *club*) is relegated to last."

On this occasion, two of his opponents failed to strengthen their original hand, one drew to a full house, but Karl managed to win by accumulating four of a kind.

Smiling at his good fortune, he undressed, took his sedative, and prepared to surrender to a cleansing sleep. Stretching out on his king-sized bed, the weary corporal closed his eyes at last and reckoned that, while he slept, all hell would continue breaking loose in Delta County.

Chapter 13

Memories

(December 31 / 6:15 a.m.)

As the hall clock struck the quarter-hour, Annie Sands stretched and yawned. She'd spent the better part of the night and early morning reading Herbert Schulz's unpublished manuscript. She'd begun hours ago by rescuing a page from the sleepy grip of her detective husband. The theme of that page and those which immediately followed had been the wartime survival story of two local elders who had recently been guests at Annie's surprise birthday party. The writing spoke of two people whom Annie loved dearly and believed she knew well.

Turns out she didn't know them quite as well as she thought she did.

The narrative revealed that Father Thomas and Caroline Liberstein shared a bittersweet past. Like Trinidad, Annie wasn't certain whether Herbert or Meeska had authored this portion of the manuscript. But whoever the writer was, it was evident that he or she was sharing facts with which they were intimately acquainted. A casual reader who was unfamiliar with the clergyman or Caroline might wonder if the account was exaggerated. But, having met and interacted with both principal subjects, Annie found the revelations entirely plausible.

Whenever Father Thomas and the widow Liberstein were together, she'd seen them exchanging what she could only characterize as "knowing looks." And more than once, she'd witnessed them touching hands and lingering in each other's presence, as if reluctant to let one another out of sight. It wasn't sexual attraction or anything approaching a romantic notion—it was a case of old friends mutually seeking and generously granting solace.

What Annie read on that winter's morning as her darling husband slumbered nearby, brought tears to her eyes. When Trinidad awoke, she'd share what she was learning. For now, she relished each word.

Though their former identities were not divulged, the writer intimated that Father Thomas and Caroline Liberstein had emigrated to America under those assumed names. During the darkest days of World War II, both had been held prisoner in a Nazi concentration camp. Both had been forced to work as slave labor in a munitions factory and they'd endured unnamed, but clearly dreadful, medical procedures. Father Thomas had fought with the Dutch resistance before he was captured, and Caroline and her husband were Jewish newlyweds who were arrested in Poland. Caroline's husband died in captivity, and, after a time, she and Thomas joined other prisoners to work on a secret project.

Odd as it seemed, Caroline and the others were put to work minting, burnishing, and sorting counterfeit American coins—five-cent pieces with a profile of the patriot and president Thomas Jefferson on one side and Jefferson's ambitious Monticello residence on the reverse. The irony of standing in an assembly line while stamping "In God We Trust" and "Liberty" on millions of metallic discs was not lost on any of the captives. Later, when adopting his alias, Father Thomas could not resist a nod to Jefferson. Nor was Caroline able to avoid adopting a surname which reflected her past practice of eternally stamping "Liberty" upon a passing parade of manufactured coins.

A few paragraphs later, Annie learned that the Nazi-manufactured coins were purposely minted at a weight which fell short of the density of a legitimate nickel. That intentional deviation was part and parcel of a diabolical German plot, the details of which she would most definitely share with Trinidad when the sleepyhead awoke.

The pages Annie was reading were photocopies and she paused as she imagined an image of Herbert Schulz laboring in the local library—inserting coin after coin into the village's one-and-only copy machine.

"Must have cost a fortune. To offset the cost, the old guy could probably have used a few of those nickels—except those bogus coins with their wonky weights wouldn't have worked," she concluded.

She turned the page and discovered an anomaly. Instead of a neatly typewritten sheet, she came across a decidedly off-center image of a newspaper clipping. She sighed as she read the details of Meeska's obituary. Herbert had copied the original obit, including a stray paper clip, and next to the black-and-white reproduction was a handwritten note: *buried both, C.B.G.—5-cents.*

"Hmm," she whispered aloud. "Give me a 'C.' Give me a 'B.' Give me a 'G.' And what does it spell? Hmm. No idea. Maybe when Rip Van Sands awakens, we can put our collective heads together. Meanwhile—"

The farmhouse's grandfather clock chimed the hour. Annie stood and stretched, then she ambled into the kitchen to start coffee brewing and search for yesterday's day-old donuts. By the time she returned to the living room balancing two steaming cups and three still-edible donuts on a tray, Trinidad had disappeared.

"Sleepwalking his way upstairs to bed," she guessed. "That's what happens when you stay up too late on a school night. Anyhow, this eliminates the need to haggle over how to fairly split up three maple-glazed donuts. So, back to work."

Before proceeding to the remaining pages, Annie took a moment to re-read the photocopied obituary and contemplate the meaning of the mysterious notation. Then she read with interest Herbert's account of the couple's early married life, their acquisition of the farm, and their child-rearing years. Herbert's loving descriptions of Meeska's daily habit of placing fresh flowers on the kitchen table caused her to pause and wipe away tears.

Such a love, she told herself.

Skimming ahead, Annie discovered a chapter devoted to the couple's decision to sell the farm and move into the village. They purchased an older home on the outskirts of Lavender—a fixer-upper Herbert admitted. But he and Meeska seemed to relish the challenge of renovating the neglected building. Soon it was a neighborhood show place.

Not anymore, Annie decided.

She hadn't driven by the old Schulz house on G Street since last summer. The once cared-for dwelling had come full circle. It had looked sad in August, and forlorn. She imagined the abandoned house would look even more desolate in the gray light of winter. Nevertheless, she'd stop by when she had a chance—just to make sure the empty building hadn't been vandalized. She'd take a look, even though the chances of someone in law-abiding Lavender damaging the old place were extremely remote.

Upstairs while his wife reviewed the Schulz manuscript, Trinidad's slumbering mind placed him in the Village of

Lavender's popular Pancake House as he and the late Herb Schulz observed a mud-caked vehicle rolling slowly through the place's parking lot. As they watched, the dull-grey vehicle seemed to dematerialize until it vanished. Then Herbert himself faded and the dream repeated. The scene seemed to be permanently etched in Trinidad's dreaming memory and it was all the more indelible because the detective had a nagging feeling that he'd seen the same nondescript vehicle more than once in the waking world.

But when and where? Trinidad asked himself. *When and where?*

Chapter 14

Trouble in Paradise
(December 31 / 7:30 a.m.)

 While Annie Sands concentrated on Herbert Schulz's unpublished manuscript and her slumbering husband dreamt of mud-caked trucks, Sheriff Jack Treadway awakened to find that young Tiff Northbridge had left their bed. Probably he'd been snoring and lately she'd grown less tolerant of his nocturnal noises. A month ago, she would have awakened him, gently chastised him, and made love. Now she'd pulled away without a sound. She'd done that before and, if the pattern held, she would have carried her pillow down to the spare bedroom and latched the door.

 Walking half-awake down the hallway, the sheriff knocked gently on the spare room door and called Tiff's name, but she didn't answer. Frustrated, he went downstairs and into the study where he sat down at his cluttered desk and turned on the gooseneck lamp.

That's when he noticed it.

For several moments, he sat there, fingering the envelope. Tuesday was typically the day he paid the bills. Just a routine he'd fallen into, no particular reason for it, just habit. Every Tuesday morning, before time to leave for work, Jack would sit at this same desk and—using the letter opener which he'd made decades ago in his high school woodshop class—he'd open the bills one-by-one and write the checks. And once a month, he'd also balance his checkbook—to the penny.

Months ago, when the couple had first begun sleeping together, Tiff had found his habits charming. Lately she'd been less tolerant.

"Why not pay the bills as they arrive?" she'd asked with a tone of exasperation. "It would make me nervous to have them all pile up like that. Aren't you afraid of sending a payment in late?"

"Never came up," he'd assured her.

She'd made a scoffing noise and walked away. In the past, when their relationship was new, she'd sit nearby as he wrestled with the bills, reading her Bible, pausing now and then to exchange a loving glance, sometimes so unable to control her ardor that she'd push the papers aside and entice him to make love to her on the desk or in a chair or on the sofa or the floor. Now, things were different. Tiff was running hot and cold—mostly cold. Cold, distant, and quick to find something to be critical about, then prone to walk away after delivering a barbed comment.

Jack should have seen it coming. Why did he not see it coming?

"No fool like an old fool," he said aloud as he fingered the envelope, recalling the many times Tiff had critiqued his posture or criticized his dress—even standing behind him to correct the tuck of his shirt. "Should'a seen it," he decided.

At last, as though dreading the task, he reached inside the envelope and extracted the contents. For a heartbeat, he hesitated, convinced that what he did next would mark the beginning of the end of this romance—a romance which he'd idiotically convinced himself would last forever. With a heavy sigh, he forced himself to do what must be done.

As he unfolded the pages and placed each one on the desk, the increasingly-unhappy sheriff could see that the three sheets, though folded together, were clearly out of order. What should have been the final sheet, the one showing his current checking and savings balances, was on top. He looked again at the envelope and then—as his hopes continued to fade—he examined the other bills. None of the other envelopes had been breached and he was certain he hadn't used the letter opener on this particular envelope—the one containing his monthly bank statement.

So, his vivacious young lover had opened the statement, looked at it, and—possibly hearing his patrol car coming up the driveway or hearing him coming out of the shower or starting downstairs—whatever had interrupted her snooping—Tiff had hurriedly reassembled the mailing. Having sneaked a look at his finances, she would have hastily restuffed the envelope and hoped, he imagined, that the doddering old fool, whom she was pleasuring now and then, at her leisure, and on a deliberate timeline of her own choosing, wouldn't remember whether or not he'd sliced the dang thing open.

"Stop it," Jack said out loud—trying to convince himself he was imagining things—but instantly recognizing that, whatever he and young Tiff had shared, it had been relentlessly unraveling. Some of his more outspoken friends had warned him that the young assistant coroner had left a string of broken hearts in metro-Denver before moving to Western Colorado where she'd managed to skewer and dump at least two additional lovers. And they had cautioned him that, in every case, these past breakups had centered on money—on Tiff's desire for security and her assessment of each man's material wealth.

Though Tiff had revealed little about her past, Jack knew something of his lover's background. Especially poignant were the things she'd revealed early on in their relationship when he awoke in the middle of the night and found the distraught woman sitting on the floor at the foot of their bed weeping uncontrollably.

"I dreamed we were poor," was all he could manage to comprehend as her voice was interrupted by gulping sobs. "I dreamed I was home again, in that old drafty house, Momma and Daddy and all us kids, and we were poor," she cried.

"I can't—I won't—I can't—oh, Honey, hold me," she insisted. "Make love to me and promise you'll always be here for me."

What else could Jack do? He promised he'd never leave her. Then he took the beautiful woman in his arms and carried her back to their bed. That had been four months ago and now he couldn't remember the last time she'd confided in him or confirmed their commitment to one another.

"Hmm," he sighed, and he forced himself to look at the balances on his statement, knowing full-well that the figures told a bleak story. He wasn't broke, but he was far from rich. A glance would've told Tiff all she needed to know. Jack sensed that their romance—their affair—their fling or whatever—was over. It was just a matter of when Tiff was going to get around to telling him.

Chapter 15

Tiff
(December 31 / 9:15 a.m.)

It was mid-morning on a Tuesday—a weekday—but Tiff Northbridge continued to feign sleep as she listened to the sounds of Jack Treadway getting ready for work. She heard muffled tones as Jack made the promised call to Trinidad. Then she pulled the covers over her head and pretended not to hear when Jack knocked again at the spare bedroom door, called her *Sweetheart,* and invited her to join him for lunch downtown.

Finally, he was gone, and the house was quiet, and she could breathe again.

For a fleeting moment she sat up in bed and leafed through her Bible and prayed to God to forgive her for what she was about to do, what she'd already done, and what she'd done before. But midway through she closed the Bible and decided it wasn't her fault. Men just fell for her, that's all there was to it. And could she help it if most of her admirers were older? She was attracted to older men for the security they seemed to offer and they, in turn, were attracted to her for obvious reasons. Was it her fault if one old fool after another didn't pan out financially?

Besides, the silly saps ought to know better.

How could they possibly believe that a woman such as herself—a woman in her sexual prime—could be satisfied with an aging lover? Well, she gave each of them a good ride. They should be grateful. They should be gracious and allow her to move on and live her life to the fullest.

Feeling she'd justified her past and current behavior, Tiff put her Bible aside and admired her body in the mirror, then she showered, dressed, and went downstairs. By the time she had eaten a hearty breakfast, she'd made up her mind. A few more not so subtle hints and Jack himself would probably come to the realization that it was over. It was always better, she'd found in the past, to let the man break it off. That was the ideal strategy, pull away a little at a time, withhold a hug here, a caress there, draw down the intimacy with subtle but relentless efficiency. But Jack was becoming a drag, so she'd have to hurry things along. The only question at present was where to land next, but it was a question she'd already considered.

Rapidly packing her things, she decided to put off telephoning her office. They'd be expecting her in today, but there would be time later to notify them that she'd be taking a few days off. Then she left a terse note on the kitchen table. In it she said she was going to visit a girlfriend—which was partially true—and that she wouldn't be back for days—also true. She added a postscript that she'd give Jack a call soon, but that, of course, was a lie. With luck she wouldn't have to interact with the sheriff any time soon. When she didn't come back, he'd surely get the hint and break things off. Then, going forward, except for being forced into each other's company in their official capacities, that would be the end of it. Also, she was certain her icy demeanor would carry her through those future encounters.

She'd be professional, keep things in proper perspective, and leave it to Jack to muddle through. She'd apologize for not knowing her heart and he'd get over it. No matter how much they claimed to love her, the men always got over it. Moreover, whether Jack did or didn't get over things, she was already past caring. That was then, this was now. She had other and bigger fish to fry.

Eventually, if things got too tense at work, he or she might have to resign and it might be her, but she'd burn that bridge when she came to it. In the meantime, she finished her note, deliberately didn't sign it, and pointedly did not draw her little smiling heart face at the bottom of the sheet.

A guy would have to be a total brick not to pick up the blatant hints contained in those glaring omissions. Meanwhile, she'd set her sights on Coal-Slide Canyon. Her friend

Judith had been away for the summer and had apparently extended her trip through autumn and into winter, but she'd probably be back any day now. In the meantime, what could be more innocent than Tiff showing up at Bistro Manor, feigning surprise not to find Judith at home, and playing her "I've always relied on the kindness of strangers" role? Her prospective target would be Judith's new man—was his name Kurt or Karl?

Whatever, Tiff told herself.

Anyhow, he was a man and he'd take Tiff into his fabulous manor and there'd be absolutely no reason for Tiff to ever return to Jack's modest two-story stick-built house. Outside in the driveway, the departing woman took a final look at the sheriff's ordinary dwelling and mentally compared it to the sprawling complex up in Coal-Slide Canyon.

Acting boldly with Judith away, Tiff would drop in this very morning and regale the lord of the manor with a sob story about how Jack had thrown her out. One good cry and, before either her unsuspecting friend or the handsome Mr. Bistro knew what hit them, Judith's temporary role as his once-favored squeeze would be history. While it was true that they were the same height and possibly shared a similar dress size, there was no way the spindly redhead could possibly compete with Tiff's sparkling blondeness. And no way could skinny Judith match Tiff's toned body with its satin-smooth skin and breathtaking features. She had Judith on breasts alone and she knew it.

To complete her plan, Tiff hurriedly sent a text to Annie Sands, asking to be excused from the New Year's Eve celebration at Lavender Hill Farm. With luck, she'd be spending that particular holiday at Bistro Manor. As she drove toward the manor, Tiff's future seemed to appear before her—flawless and tailor-made and profitable. Using her sexuality, Tiff would soon squeeze Judith out of the picture and, with the competition sent packing, she'd take up residence in the manor. Then, in no time at all, she was certain she'd be sweating and moaning in three-quarter time as her smitten host busted a gut to pleasure her.

If Tiff played her cards right, this would be the very last time she'd have to put-out to achieve financial security, because she was dead certain that Mr. Bistro would, finally, be the one she'd cling to. After all, the macho man was much closer to her age—just three years older as she recalled—and his body seemed sound and so, thank God, did his bank account. There was no need to sneak a peek at Bistro's financial statements, the man practically exuded money.

In Tiff's mind, as she passed Brimstone Corner, left the main pavement, and started up the Canyon road, she saw herself marrying well and living happily ever-after and if Sheriff Jack didn't like it—well, that was *his* problem.

Chapter 16

Into the Spider's Parlor
(December 31 / 11:00 a.m.)

Karl Bistro placed a rum and coke in front of his guest and then took a seat in the chair opposite. Tiff Northbridge sipped the drink demurely, glancing coyly in his direction, displaying a pair of bright blue eyes. Karl stared back with his dark eyes, certain that Tiff's puppy-dog look was a calculated maneuver and thinking that he knew how to bust a few moves of his own. Which was why, instead of boldly sitting beside her on the comfortable couch which would conveniently place their hips within striking distance, he'd opted to sit nearby—but not too close—in a vintage wing chair.

"Tell me more," Karl prompted.

"There's nothing else to tell," she said.

"So, you say that our Boy Scout of a sheriff was mean to you and tossed you out?"

"Not exactly *mean*," she corrected. "I never said Jack was abusive. He just put too much pressure on me by asking me to marry him and I just didn't see it happening, that's all."

"You did not see marrying a public servant on a government salary. Is that it?"

"Well, yes, there's that," she admitted. *Why not tell this man the truth?* she thought. *That way I won't have to go to all the trouble of remembering yet another story.* "Plus, he's older, you know, much too old for me."

"A bit like Judith and I," Karl offered.

"Sort of," Tiff said and then she laughed. "Except it's just the opposite."

"How so?"

"It's not a case of you being too old for Judith," she declared. "It's more a case of *her* being too young for *you*."

"You have a point there," he agreed. "In fact, I think I can safely say—without the least fear of contradiction— that young Judith will never grow up."

"So, you see what I mean," she said, telling herself that this was going to be easier than she thought. "The age thing—whichever way it happens—it's a deal-breaker."

There was an awkward silence during which Tiff could hear the ticking of the antique grandfather clock which commanded the front hall of Bistro Manor. All at once the clock mechanisms whirled as the instrument struck the quarter hour and the unfamiliar sound made Tiff jump.

"Jeepers!" she exclaimed. "That will take some getting used to."

"As I said," Karl noted, "you are welcome to stay here at the manor while you sort things out."

"You're certain Judith won't mind?" Tiff asked.

"I guarantee she will not object," said Karl.

There was another silence during which Tiff began to feel uneasy.

"When did you say Judith is due back?" Tiff asked.

"I did not say," Karl crooned as he sat his drink down and crossed over to sit beside Tiff. "In fact, I doubt that she is coming back." He took Tiff's drink from her hand and placed it on the coffee table. "Shall we?" And with that, he pushed Tiff down on the couch until she was lying on her back. She felt suddenly drowsy and didn't resist. "Close your eyes please," Karl said. She obeyed and her mind collapsed before she could process another thought.

Chapter 17

Collateral Damage
(December 31 / Early Evening)

Sheriff Jack Treadway had fallen hard for the vivacious and coquettish Tiff Northbridge, the new young medical examiner who was twenty years his junior.

They'd conducted a torrid autumn romance which had lasted until early December. That's when Tiff confided in Annie Sands that Jack had surprised and alarmed her by proposing marriage.

"We had our fun," she'd told Annie. "But I have no confidence in him as a prospective husband and I've got to move on."

When Trinidad mentioned that Jack and Tiff seemed to be experiencing a rough patch, Annie sensed that the end of the relationship was imminent. When New Year's Eve loomed on the horizon, she couldn't keep her suspicions to herself any longer. Like it or not, Trinidad had to be told.

"Did you notice that Jack's on our invite list for tonight?" Annie asked as the couple stood in their upstairs bedroom, changing outfits in anticipation of their coming New Year's Eve party. "But not Tiff?" she added.

"I noticed," Trinidad said. "So, what gives?"

"Being excluded was her request," said Annie.

"Hmm," he said. "You interest me strangely. Is there something I ought to know?"

Feeling guilty for withholding the secret for so long, Annie told Trinidad what Tiff had said about having no confidence in Jack as a prospective husband. Hearing this seemingly contrived excuse, Trinidad had a strong reaction.

"No confidence in him as a husband? Ain't that woman-speak for Jack doesn't make enough money and young Tiff is on the prowl for a rich spouse?"

"Cynic," Annie chastised.

"Realist," Trinidad countered. "Believe me, I've been there."

"Since when?" Annie asked and she couldn't suppress her laugh. "I hear from your Mom that, in your wild and younger days, you were more likely to be the heartbreaker than the victim of love."

"I don't suppose my mother mentioned Paige," Trinidad said.

"Paige? You mean Paige Turner, that floozy of an exotic dancer you had the boyhood crush on?"

"The very same," Trinidad said, and it was his turn to smile.

"Honestly, I don't see the connection," Annie said.

"Ms. Turner was thirty-four years of age," he said. "And I—her secret admirer—was all of fourteen. So, there's your twenty-year age gap."

"Well," said Annie. "It's an unbelievable stretch to compare your adolescent obsession over a four-color, six-foot-tall music-hall poster with the trials and tribulations of two flesh-and-blood people—both friends of ours by the way—and both of whom, as far as I can tell, will suffer over this break-up."

"Jack will suffer, yes," Trinidad observed. "But I don't see Tiff carrying a torch."

"She's young and more resilient," Annie said without conviction.

"She's young alright, but also old enough to know better than to toy with a grown man's affections," Trinidad said.

"He didn't seem to mind it at the time," she argued.

"That's because Jack fell in love and he believed it would last," he countered.

"May-December romances are doomed from the get-go," she said.

"They are when one party is in love and the other one is just taking a side road in her search for a meal ticket," Trinidad said. "And I really don't want to talk about this anymore."

"Then why the heck did you bring it up in the first place?" she sounded incredulous.

"I thought you started this," he recalled.

"Now you're making me feel bad," she said.

"Sorry," he apologized. "It's just that Jack's an old friend and I hate to see him sad. But my concern about him is no reason for me to get all-up on your case or make you feel bad. After all it's not your fault they broke up."

"The truth is it's nobody's fault. It's just one of those things that need to work themselves out. Now, we'll just have time before the guests arrive, so why not turn off the light and make love to me?" Annie suggested. "Somehow that always seems to brighten my mood."

"That sounds to me like a fine idea," Trinidad agreed as he switched off the bedside lamp and proceeded to do his best to follow his charming bride's instructions.

Chapter 18

Dig
(December 31 / 11:45 p.m.)

While Tiff Northbridge remained incapacitated in a narcotic-induced slumber, Corporal Karl Bistro left his manor and embarked upon a mission to dig up a cadaver. It wasn't his first time. It was not, as the American's say, his first rodeo. It was, however, the first time he'd been obliged to use heavy equipment to complete the job. The dead of night and the quiet incisions of a garden spade were more his cup of tea.

Another idiom, he told himself. *The English language is such a minefield of idioms, phrases, metaphors, similes, axioms, slogans, allegories, adages, proverbs, parables, and sayings. Is it any wonder that foreign speakers struggle to comprehend?*

In any event, the wintertime ground was too frozen to allow for the use of a shovel. He'd need a more powerful tool.

Karl could have rented a backhoe, but that process would have generated a paper trail—the bane of a clandestine operative such as himself. It had been far easier and more prudent to steal the sturdy apparatus—an option which required, among other things, the practical application of bolt cutters. Locating an unguarded site containing both the machine and the trailer needed to transport it turned out to be child's play. In fact, a child could have managed it, providing that child could sever the requisite number of chains and padlock shanks, latch a trailer coupler to a hitch ball, and reach the pedals to drive the getaway truck.

Stealing the equipment trailer and backhoe from a secluded and unsupervised worksite was one thing. Digging up a healthy rectangle of cemetery soil and the probability of having to penetrate a burial vault was something else again. Under ideal circumstances, the business of illegally unearthing a body required single-minded boldness, stealth, and darkness. Midnight offered cover but also raised the complication of noise.

Our Lady of Mercy Catholic Cemetery was isolated but there were farmhouses near enough for the racket of the chugging backhoe to disturb even the soundest sleeper. Moreover, people might be up late to greet the New Year. On the other hand, the din of fireworks and similar celebratory commotions could generate sufficient distractions to mask Karl's labors. In any event, the decisive corporal planned to move rapidly and with a minimum of noise. He'd make quick work of disinterring the coffin and he'd also have the luxury of leaving the casket exposed and the hole uncovered, which would reduce the time on task and limit the risk of being detected.

If it were done when 'tis done, then 'twere well it were done quickly! Karl recalled that old chestnut, though he'd forgotten the author.

Arriving at Our Lady's, he overcame the unwelcome chore of hauling the purloined backhoe through a trio of tight corners and up the steep dirt track which led from the pavement to the cemetery. But he managed it. Once on top, he discovered that his target wasn't near the narrow roadway which bisected the graveyard. Undaunted and without a moment's hesitation, he accelerated and drove straight over the frosty grounds—gouging a destructive path and damaging headstones as he went.

Reaching the spot, he offloaded the backhoe, unhitched the trailer, and set to work removing earth. Within a matter of minutes, he reached the concrete vault, crashed through, and used the machine's claw-like bucket and an improvised sling to extract the coffin. Seconds later, he shut the apparatus down. He'd estimated that—once he began digging—the extraction would take twenty minutes. He did it in twelve.

In anticipation of locating a hidden cache of war nickels, he'd stowed a wheelbarrow and other essential tools in the truck bed. But, upon using a crowbar to pry the casket open as well as inserting himself into the empty hole to scan the cavity with a metal detector, he discovered that the grave contained nothing more than advertised on the headstone: *Meeska Schulz: 1927-2009: O for the touch of a vanish'd hand. And the sound of a voice that is still.*

Karl was unmoved by the sentimental inscription. The unscrupulous corporal had no qualms about disturbing the dead. For him, this brazen exhumation was an absolutely necessary and purely unemotional reaction to the clue contained in a particular chapter of Herbert Schulz's manuscript—a rambling account of the old man's life which Karl had lifted from the Delta County Sheriff's evidence locker.

A few days ago, acting on instructions from his master, Karl had stolen the evidence document. Posing as an FBI agent by flashing one of his many expertly-forged identification cards, Karl had taken the manuscript and signed *Rumpelstiltskin*. The officer on duty didn't bother to match his signature with his ID or otherwise attempt to decipher his scrawl. Karl supposed that someone would eventually be disciplined for that oversight.

Though the manuscript was incomplete, it included a newspaper clipping of Meeska's obituary containing the name of the officiating undertaker and place of burial. A handwritten notation in the margin read: *buried both, C.B.G.—5-cents.*

To the corporal, those initials suggested "Catholic Burial Ground," and, in his opinion, the five-cents remark was self-explanatory. That impression was further reinforced by other references in the sample chapters which seemed to equate Schulz's late wife with the war nickels.

Regardless of Karl's expectations, the unearthing had been a disappointment. But since the corporal was leaving everything behind—empty trailer, stolen backhoe, defiled casket, and cemetery damage—that theft and his wanton desecration would generate additional mysteries to distract the authorities. He could see the headlines now. Too bad the local newspapers were both weekly publications, but it wasn't the population in general that Karl was striving to bamboozle. It was the sheriff and that plodding man's allies who were the targets of his campaign of chaos. Tonight's damage would, he was certain, cause his adversaries to be alarmed and thus further perplexed by the time the rooster crowed.

Intent on heightening his malicious vandalism, Karl spun the Toyota's wheels, spewing frozen mud and dull tufts of grass into the frosty air. As the truck careened over the snow-covered ground, he spotted the cemetery flagpole and sped toward it. He braked just short of the base, leapt from the truck, and hauled down the flag.

"One more poke in the sheriff's eye," the corporal said aloud as he unhooked the banner.

When he reached the entry gate, he was tempted to ram his way out. But he was unwilling to risk damaging his

Toyota. So, he stopped, left the motor running, got out, and pushed the wrought iron barrier aside. The ancient gate creaked on its hinges. Returning to his truck, he drove through the opening and stepped out, intending to close the gate.

But open is better, he told himself as he left the gate ajar. *Open is an invitation to see what is amiss.*

Then, rather than driving away, he paused to examine the star-studded sky. The anemic light of the new moon did little to diminish the dark void. He had learned his constellations in school—ages ago. Though it was risky to tarry, he lingered and rotated from northeast to southwest, noting the star clusters as he pivoted in place: Ursa Major, Big Dipper, Cassiopeia, Cepheus, Perseus, Orion—the major December constellations.

At last, he eased back into his truck and headed home. Glancing at his watch, he calculated that his newly-acquired houseguest would be partially awake but still groggy enough to yield to his erotic desires.

"It is good to be alive," he said aloud.

Chapter 19

Two Beers
(January 1, 2020 / 2:00 a.m.)

"There's no fool like an old fool," Sheriff Jack Treadway repeated the self-deprecating critique as he nursed his beer.

He and Trinidad Sands were sitting in the front room of the Lavender Hill farmhouse with the lights off as a healthy blaze roared in the fireplace.

"How many is that now?" Trinidad asked, trying to make the question sound casual, hoping the concern wasn't evident in his voice. The other guests had tottered off into the frigid night and Annie had also turned in, but not before giving her husband a not-so-subtle hint to keep Jack in the living room and talking.

"What if he doesn't want to talk about it?" Trinidad protested.

"Then you do the talking," she said.

The challenge of discussing emotions might have been an insurmountable chore for both men. But armed with a caring mandate from his wise and lovely wife, Trinidad had decided to stick it out. So, the detective threw another log on the fire and tried to keep the conversation going.

"How many is that?" Trinidad asked again.

"You want to know how many," said Jack. "And, in response to your question, I say two beers so far—and my absolute limit is three."

"Since when?"

"Since this," Jack pulled Tiff's crumbled note from his pocket, fingered it for a moment, and then put it back.

Am I ever going to find out what's written on that wretched paper? Trinidad asked himself.

"So, look, I get it—you got a note—" Trinidad prompted, but his morose friend just stared at the fire and seemed not to hear.

"My heart ain't caught up to my head yet," Jack said. "That's it in a miserable nutshell. I was out there on that old bench yesterday afternoon. The park bench right by the lake, you know? Just out there in the cold. I was out there on that bench where me and Tiff first told our love for one another. That time when we made that promise was in August. I looked out at the horizon that day, and I recall the sun was just dawnin' and so I remember that-there moment as the start of somethin' new and special. But all that while, I didn't understand what it all really meant."

Jack halted then and his voice faltered. He seemed about to weep, but he lowered his head and covered his eyes with his good hand. For a time, the two men sat side-by-side in silence.

"I—" Trinidad began.

"Hell, I know I ain't perfect and I know I ain't the brightest bulb in the county, but if only I'd realized what I should'a knowed in August. Here I was on that dang bench and thinkin' I saw a sunrise and the start of things, while right beside me on that self-same little bench was Tiff who seen the whole thing as the total opposite. I seen it as a sunrise whereas she seen it as a sunset—as the end of things, not the start. Knowin' what I know now, I gotta believe that, even when she said she loved me, she was, right then-and-there, calculatin' her escape."

"Jack," Trinidad said, "I know you're not perfect—nobody is. But—"

"So, what did I do tonight when I got this—this—this—" He paused and struggled to get the note out of whichever pocket he'd placed it in. "This—this-here dang note. And what did I do when I got it? Tell me again, Slick, exactly what did I do?"

"You punched her picture," Trinidad reminded his friend.

"Dang-straight," said Jack holding up his bandaged hand. "Right through the ever-lovin' glass. Boom! And, man oh man, I'm here to tell you, that punch made for one whole heck of a terrible lot of blood."

The two men were silent as Trinidad wondered what to say to a guy who got a Dear Jack note and punched his hand through an 8 x 10 pane of cut glass.

"I reckon that's enough whinin' for one New Year's," Jack said. "So, how's about you get me that last final beer?"

Chapter 20

Three Beers
(January 1 / 4:00 a.m.)

After drinking his third beer, Sheriff Jack Treadway had called a taxi to carry him back to Delta City. It had already been a long night. So, Trinidad and Annie Sands were surprised to hear ringing in the pre-dawn darkness. Several minutes passed while Trinidad stumbled out of bed and trundled downstairs to answer the kitchen phone.

"Where are you, Jack? Just tell me where you are," Trinidad was sitting at the kitchen table as Annie joined her husband and placed both hands on his shoulders for moral support.

"Listen to this," said Jack and his voice on the phone sounded hollow. There was a pause, but that gap was only filled with silence.

"I don't hear anything," Trinidad said.

"Not yet," said Jack. "I sent you a file. It ought'a be there soon unless your crappy cellphone don't pick it up."

"I'm on our landline," said Trinidad. "But Annie will head upstairs to check my cell—"

"No women!" Jack cursed. "No women—this is just between us men, understand?"

"Come on, Jack," said Trinidad. "You know you can trust Annie. We only want to help."

"Okay then—Annie's okay. But no 'nother women," Jack decided. "So, listen to the files and I'll call you back."

"Files—?" Trinidad began, but the line went dead.

Annie rushed upstairs to try getting a signal on the cellphone. Trinidad followed her and hurriedly dressed.

"Can we ping his phone to see where he is?" she asked.

"Probably not and I'm not sure we'll be able to see, let alone hear, the files he's sending," said Trinidad as he pulled on his boots. "And files? What files is he talking about? And anyway, I have a pretty good idea of where he is. You stay here to call him back and keep him talking."

"Where are you going?" Annie shouted as her husband started downstairs. "Where's Jack?"

"The bench," Trinidad yelled as he reached the front door. "He's gotta be out there on the bench."

Chapter 21

Call Back
(January 1 / 4:30 a.m.)

Left behind at Lavender Hill Farm while her husband rushed out into the dark, Annie Sands hurriedly punched in Sheriff Jack Treadway's cellphone number and waited anxiously while it rang five times. At last, Jack answered.

"Is that you, Annie?" Jack asked in a tone which sounded so sad that it nearly broke her heart.

"Yes, it's me," Annie answered. "Are you okay?"

"Never better. Did you get them audio files I sent over?"

"Yes, I got them."

"Did you listen to them?"

"Yes."

"And—?"

"Jack, I don't know what to say. Except to say that you should've erased those. Keeping them is a bad idea—"

"Honey Girl, didn't I tell you?"

"Tell me what, Jack?"

"I thought I *had* erased them and then this morning a little thingy pops up—you know—one of those little doodads on the phone?"

"Do you mean an icon?" Annie asked.

"Bingo," Jack confirmed. "So, this little acorn thing is blinkin' and I punch it and up comes this here whatchamacallit—like at the restaurant—you know?"

"Menu? A menu popped up?"

"Yeah—a menu—and it says I got five songs saved."

"Oh no—" Annie began. "You didn't—"

"Didn't I just?" Jack said and he managed a chuckle.

"Oh, Jack—"

"I pushed number one and what do you think I heard?" the sheriff asked.

"Jack—"

"Punch it and see—" he insisted.

"Jack, I already did that—"

"Punch it please," Jack pleaded. "Punch it again."

"Okay," said Annie. *Anything,* she thought, *to keep Jack talking until Trinidad gets there.* Annie punched the file and Tiff's voice sounded over the cellphone's tinny speaker.

"Honey," the recording said, "I just had to call and tell you how very, very much I love you. I *do* love you with all my heart and I can't wait until—"

"Jack, I—" Annie said as she paused the audio.

"All the way to the end," Jack said. "Let it play out."

"Okay," said Annie.

"—we're together again. Anyway, I'm counting the moments until I can hold you again," Tiff's voice continued sounding so genuine, so sincere. "Anyhow, I'm starting to blabber so bye-bye and don't forget the ice cream. See you soon—all my love, Sweetheart."

Jack was silent and Annie was searching for words to say.

"Jack, you really, really need to delete these—all of them."

"I know," said Jack and his voice sounded small. "I already done that on this end. I just wanted somebody else to hear it—just so they'd know I wasn't crazy."

"Jack, nobody thinks you're—"

"So, these-here lost and found voicemails prove I wasn't crazy, see? I was startin' to think I imagined that she loved me. That I imagined the whole thing—that it never happened. But this proves I ain't crazy—she *did* love me, once anyway."

"Jack," Annie pleaded, "don't torture yourself like this."

"Oh, don't you worry," said Jack and she could hear a bit of his old self. "Strange as it seems, these-here messages from the past really helped me snap out of it. Just understandin' that I hadn't been foolin' myself makes all the difference. So, do me a favor and erase your end too, okay? I don't never want to hear that voice again."

"Already done, pal," Annie said. "Now—"

"Well, I gotta run," said Jack. "Your husband just showed up."

And Jack ended the call before Annie could say another word.

Chapter 22

Park Bench at the Edge of the World
(January 1 / 6:00 a.m.)

    Trinidad Sands found Sheriff Jack Treadway exactly where he expected. The questing detective located the troubled sheriff sitting alone on a park bench overlooking Delta City's Confluence Lake. The lake was frozen solid except for a patch of open water near the inlet where a score of noisy geese had gathered. The Gunnison River was flowing nearby, its dark surface dotted with chunks of ice as it rushed beneath a narrow footbridge. A swirling fog shrouded the bridge in a rising mist so dense that its far end appeared to vanish into a low-hanging cloud.

    Jack had his back to the road as Trinidad parked his Ridgeline. The detective walked across the frozen ground and approached the bench from behind. Purposely crunching his footsteps in the frozen snow to let Jack know someone was coming, Trinidad walked forward until he was close enough to see a service revolver lying un-holstered on the seat beside his friend.

"Jack," he said and when the sheriff didn't respond, Trinidad said his name again.

"You here?" Jack asked.

"I saw your patrol car," said Trinidad as he sat down beside his friend and allowed his left hand to stray a few inches toward the pistol. "You know your motor's running."

"Protocol," said the sheriff without further explanation.

"'Tain't that cold out," observed Trinidad.

"Not below-zero protocol," said Jack. "Suicide watch—" his voice trailed off.

"Jack, I—" Trinidad began.

"Oh, hell, it ain't me," Jack said with a laugh. It was a sound that Trinidad had sorely missed these last few weeks. "Over yonder," Jack added, and he gestured toward the footbridge.

Looking closer through the swirling fog and gathering dawn, Trinidad could make out the silhouette of a rotund man in a slicker and cowboy hat.

"Not again?" Trinidad wondered aloud.

"Third time this winter," said Jack.

"Cold weather and dark days have been hard for Fingers Heckleson," Trinidad allowed as he took a closer look at the weapon on the bench between them and realized that it had to be the ranger's long-barreled pistol. Apparently the old, retired ranger had surrendered his sidearm to Jack before climbing out onto the bridge—a stunt he'd been pulling since winter set in. "It's been hard on us all," Trinidad added.

"That's one hell of an understatement," said Jack.

"I hear you cussing again," said Trinidad. "And that gives me hope."

"Yeah," said Jack. "That's my old self talkin' and old prissy-britches Tiff wouldn't of stood for that kind'a rough talk on my part for sure."

"Sarcasm," said Trinidad, "the last bastion of scoundrels."

"I loved that gal, Slick," said Jack. "Loved her most and best. Love her now still and always will, I reckon."

"That's hard, I know," said Trinidad and he was tempted to reach over and put his arm around the shoulders of his distraught friend until he thought better of it. "If my Annie was here, she'd tell you to snap out of it, but I'm pretty sure she'd also give you a hug."

"Might just work, might just be what the doctor ordered, not the hug I mean, but for you to tell me to snap out of it," Jack observed.

"The illumination's kind'a bad out here," said Trinidad. "In this dawn's early light, I can't tell if you're serious or not."

"You and your missus both bein' such good lookers, you probably don't know how it feels to be an ordinary fella when a beauty takes a shine to you until then she don't and walks away. It's like every sappy love song on the radio is all of a sudden about you and—" Jack paused and seemed to falter.

"I—" Trinidad ventured a comment but paused, unable to find the words.

"Here's the thing," Jack sniffed. "Somebody—and it might as well be you and it might as well be here and now—somebody needs to tell me, in no uncertain terms, to snap out of it," said Jack. "Can you do that for a pal?"

"Sure, I can—" Trinidad began, then he abruptly halted to shout, "Ah hell!"

Both the detective and the sheriff cursed aloud as they scrambled to their feet. While they'd been content to chatter away about broken hearts and lost love, Texas Ranger Emeritus Dallas Heckleson (known affectionately to his friends as "Fingers") had taken a header off the footbridge and made an undignified dent in the ice-crusted Gunnison River.

"Didn't think you'd do it," Jack shouted as he and Trinidad broke through the shore ice and waded out into the freezing current to tow the giant man to safety.

"Had to try it just once," sputtered the ranger. "I didn't mind the fall so much but can't truly say as I enjoyed that-there sudden stop at the bottom. I'm glad y'all showed up. Remember—y'all can pick your nose and you can pick your friends, but you can't pick your friend's nose."

"You old fool," said Jack.

"Takes one to know one," Fingers critiqued. "Dang me. What I wouldn't give just this minute fer a warm blonde, a shot of bourbon, and a nice dry blanket."

"Nuts to the blonde," said Jack.

"Amen to that," the ranger agreed.

"I'll abstain on the blonde, pass on the bourbon, and vote for the blanket," said Trinidad.

"Amen to that also," the ranger assented.

As Trinidad bundled Ranger Heckleson in one of the county's mylar emergency blankets, Jack's patrol car radio crackled.

"Base calling one, over!" the dispatcher's voice sounded urgent. At that same moment, a pair of distance sirens penetrated the early morning darkness.

"Somebody's life is changin'," Fingers observed.

"Treadway," Jack responded.

"Cemetery trouble, Boss," the dispatcher reported. "Units on their way forthwith."

"S.O.C.?" Jack asked to clarify the scene of the crime.

"Our Lady's," said the dispatcher.

"How bad, Sharon?" Jack inquired.

"Breaking and entering, vandalism, desecration—the whole nine yards."

"On my way," said Jack. "One—out. Welcome to the New Year," he told the others. "Slick, can you get Fingers home? I need to go see what's up at Our Lady's."

"Glad to oblige," said Trinidad and he helped the old ranger to his feet.

Chapter 23

Another Morning After
(January 1 / 7:00 a.m.)

There was a knock on the door and Tiff Northbridge awoke to see Karl Bistro enter the manor bedroom carrying a breakfast tray.

"Happy New Year," he beamed. "I thought you might like a bit of nourishment."

"Lovely," she said as she placed a luxurious pillow behind her back and sat up in the spacious king-sized bed. "Do you treat all your guests this way?"

"Only the ones whom I hope to see naked from time to time," he answered, and he sported a wolfish grin as he positioned the tray.

"That," she purred, "will be my pleasure after I have dined."

"You expect me to sit here calmly and watch you eat breakfast in the nude?"

"Yes, I absolutely expect you to behave until I've eaten my fill," she playfully insisted.

"That is a tall order," he said as he untied his bathrobe and let it drop to the floor. "Here I come—ready or not."

A half-hour later, Tiff lay in the wreckage of breakfast and wondered how the bed was ever going to get clean again. She'd only had a moment to gulp down a swig of orange juice before Karl pulled the covers back. In short order, the toast had been hopelessly crumpled and there were slivers of bacon everywhere and she was fairly certain she was lying on a blanket of scrambled eggs.

The lovemaking—such as it was—was brief and, for Tiff, unsatisfying. Karl was unapologetic. He carried her to the bathroom where they made love in the shower—twice—and eventually managed to scrub themselves clean. Karl left her to savor the last of the hot water while he toweled off and went to his room. When Tiff emerged from the bathroom fifteen minutes later, she was mildly surprised to see that her bed had been stripped and remade with fresh linen. She was just pulling her slacks on when the person she supposed to be the housemaid appeared with a vacuum.

"Okay, I should do this now?" the woman asked.

"Absolutely," said Tiff. "And thank you so much."

Despite receiving permission, the woman stood in the doorway.

"You'll be Miss Judith's friend," she said. It wasn't a question.

"Yes," said Tiff. "She and I are good friends.

"If you say so," said the woman as she placed the vacuum inside the door. "I'll get the bathroom first if you don't care."

"That would be lovely," said Tiff as she reached for her purse. "Do you—?" She was about to ask if the woman required a tip, but she thought better of it.

It's not as if I'm in a frigging hotel, she reminded herself.

While her purse was open, Tiff fingered her cellphone, intending to call her office and make excuses. But a tantalizing aroma made her change her mind. Leaving her purse, phone, and blouse behind, she threw on a bathrobe, started downstairs, followed her nose, and discovered another breakfast—a proper one—set out at the end of a huge table in the expansive dining room. Her host stood up to greet her and ushered her to a high-backed chair.

"Aren't you full of surprises," she smiled as she gave him a kiss.

"You have no idea," Karl said as he placed a napkin on her lap and let his hand linger there.

Chapter 24

Closet

(January 1 / 8:00 a.m.)

Feeling fatigued after yet another bout of morning lovemaking, Tiff was lounging in the upstairs bed while Karl lingered in the shower.

Clean and randy, she thought of Karl and his firm body. *That seems like an ideal combination.*

Nevertheless, she had to admit she'd been enormously relieved when at last he'd sated himself for a final time and left the room to take a shower. Meanwhile, she still hadn't had breakfast. On the ground floor, the hall clock struck the quarter hour and the chimes seemed to fill the upper story. Thinking about the clock and the sexual appetite of her newly acquired lover, Tiff told herself that there were now *two things* in this luxurious Bistro Manor which would take some getting used to: that clamorous clock and her seemingly insatiable host.

"Get dressed," Karl said as he emerged from the bathroom, crossed to the bedroom door, and disappeared into the upstairs hallway. It sounded like an order and Tiff felt compelled to obey. The room was chilly as she threw off her blankets and began to pull on her clothes. Her luggage was still in her car so, for the time being, she'd have to wear yesterday's outfit. She was just buttoning her blouse when she had a thought.

Everything else in this well-ordered household had been efficiently managed, so she found herself wondering if one of the servants might have already secured her luggage and unpacked her bags. With a tentative feeling which surprised her—a feeling that she was snooping—she crossed to the walk-in closet, turned on the wall switch, and rolled the door aside.

As she had anticipated, her clothes were already there—everything she owned neatly hanging near the door. Someone had even arranged her many shoes along the closet floor. There was no sign of her luggage, but that didn't concern her. What did concern her was what else she found in the expansive closet. The rows beyond her things were filled with other garments including a unique electric-blue party dress which she recognized as belonging to Judith.

Why, the curious young woman asked herself, *has Judith left so many of her things behind? Especially this dress—I know she dearly loves this outfit.*

Tiff reached out and fingered the luminous sleeve and she was just pondering the meaning of encountering the unexpected dress when the closet light was suddenly extinguished, and she sensed someone entering behind her. Before she could turn around, a pad of gauze was pressed over her nose and mouth while a muscular arm gripped her waist. A cloying aroma made her eyes water and the last thing she recalled before losing consciousness was Karl's voice saying, "Sleep now—sleep."

Chapter 25

Our Lady's
(January 1 / 9:00 a.m.)

Sheriff Jack Treadway stood near the flagpole at Our Lady of Mercy Catholic Cemetery. The sun was barely up, and a chill wind troubled the flag's lanyard, causing the rope to bang noisily against the metal pole. Without looking, Jack reached out to steady the twirling rope.

"Haul it down," he told the nearest deputy.

"Yes, sir," the deputy responded. "Who'd do a thing like that? Makes you wonder."

"Dire distress," Jack mumbled.

"Pardon?" the deputy inquired.

"Just get it down and make it right-side-up," Jack growled.

"Roger that," said the deputy.

Jack left the flagpole and walked to the spot where Lieutenant Madge Oxford had erected an incident tent. As he walked, the sheriff considered the deputy's question about who was behind this willful devastation. Flying the American flag upside down had to be someone sending a message and the desecration of Meeska Schulz's grave meant that particular someone was most likely her husband's killer. As for the message, Jack had to believe it was the assassin's way of saying: *I'm in your county and I'm here to wreak havoc and there isn't thing-one you can do about it.*

"Where to start with this unholy mess?" Lieutenant Madge Oxford asked as Jack joined her.

"Can't wait for the medical examiner," Jack decided.

Madge raised an eyebrow. It didn't escape her notice that the sheriff hadn't used Tiff Northbridge's name.

"Let's get Meeska back into the ground," Jack ordered. "I've got a short-handled gravel shovel in the trunk. So should you and the other patrol cars. Put Woody on the backhoe to load it onto the trailer and have him call dispatch to see if anybody's reported it missing. Least we can do right now is get it back to the owners. Everybody else on the shovels."

"Roger that," Madge said.

"I've got a naggin' feelin' that whatever the hell-heck is goin' on, it's about to get a hell of a lot worse," Jack grumbled.

"You're cussing again, Boss?" Madge asked.

"Damn right," Jack affirmed.

Chapter 26

Liberstein

(January 1 / 9:30 a.m.)

A coded text from Karl Bistro's master had revealed the aliases of his remaining targets. The sparsely populated vastness of Western Colorado would ordinarily complicate the task of locating specific individuals but narrowing the search to the Village of Lavender simplified things. No need to wonder how those identities had been discovered. The trusting corporal had long ago ceased to question the accuracy of his resourceful master.

Karl pulled over to review the informative text. Then he glanced in the backseat to make certain Tiff Northbridge wasn't stirring. He may have tied her up a bit too tight and her circulation might be constricted, but that would be the least of her problems. She was still unconscious and stretched out on the floor. As he'd been maneuvering over snowbound roads, the blanket had slipped and only a corner of it remained in place covering her face while the rest had fallen aside, exposing her prostrate body.

For a moment, he indulged a fantasy. Among his many masochistic tendencies, Karl was into bondage and, if more pressing matters hadn't been distracting him, he would have pulled over and ravaged the helpless woman. As it was, he merely reached behind and pulled the blanket back into place.

"Out of sight and out of roving mind," the determined corporal said aloud as he put the Tacoma in gear and turned off the highway. His onboard navigation system was barking out turn-by-turn commands as he rolled over snowy side roads, zigzagging for seemingly endless miles around dormant farm fields. At last, he spotted the rural mailbox he was seeking and turned sharply, skidding sideways, clipping the box with his front fender, and toppling it.

"*Verdammt,*" he cursed as he straightened his wheels, aimed for a break in the fence line, and fish-tailed onto a primitive driveway. As he drove down the steadily descending road toward the distant farmhouse, he glanced at his holstered Walther pistol positioned on the passenger seat beside him. His rifle was also nearby, propped up at an angle, with the butt of its protective case resting on the passenger-side floorboard.

Next to these weapons lay a nondescript envelope. Maybe there would be no need to risk sending the letter. Maybe this woman calling herself Caroline Liberstein would have the answers he was seeking. If not, the contents of the envelope—when delivered into the correct hands—would further stir the pot, he was certain of that.

He looked up in time to see Mrs. Liberstein emerging from the compact two-story house with a quizzical expression on her face, a heavy parka buttoned beneath her chin, and a double-barreled shotgun in her arms. Striding onto the porch with an air of determination, she was immediately followed by a huge mangy looking animal that might have been a dog or perhaps a small bear.

"*Gewiss*," he breathed aloud in German. "Of course," he translated for no one in particular. "With the death of Herr Schulz, this crafty old woman will have already anticipated my arrival."

He would expect no less of the widow of Otto Vogel. The resolute corporal smiled through the windshield as he wheeled the Tacoma into the broad farmyard. Maintaining eye contact with the woman, he nodded his head politely while steering with his left hand and using his unseen right to unsnap the keeper on his holster and insert the weapon into his waistband. He'd park far enough away to discourage the armed woman from examining the backseat and then he'd move on foot until he was within pistol range of the porch.

He turned off his ignition and exited the Tacoma, carefully buttoning his heavy coat in order to obscure the deadly

9-mm. He'd pour on the charm, put the woman at ease, and ask his questions. If the interview went well and he got what he wanted, his work would be complete. Either way, he'd kill her and probably also the dog, in whatever order the situation demanded.

"Good day," the advancing corporal called as he crunched through the snow. "Do I have the pleasure of addressing Gerda Vogel, the wife of Otto Vogel?"

Hearing those long-suppressed names, Caroline shuddered then squared her shoulders, took a step back toward her front door, and signaled the dog to take a position on the steps, forming a barrier between herself and the steadily advancing stranger. Anyone invoking those names from her tragic past was not to be trusted. This stranger's haughty demeanor and his barely detectable accent were unmistakable incarnations of her wartime nightmares.

"Far enough," she shouted, but the man kept coming. "Stop I said," she commanded.

Ignoring the woman's ultimatum, Karl walked two more steps. Then he halted and held up his left hand but kept his right close to his waist and parallel with his hidden pistol.

"Please," he said, "I only wish to talk."

"Talk from there," she said raising the shotgun—an action which caused the dog to bare its teeth and emit a low growl.

"Fine," Karl agreed. "But can you call off your dog? *Bitter*—" he added the German for please.

"This dog understands German," said Mrs. Liberstein. "And he stays put. So, say your piece. Speak up or else take one more step this way and I'll blow your trespassing behind to Kingdom Come because I'm unlikely to miss at this range."

It is also within pistol range, Karl thought to himself. But aloud he said, "As you wish. However, I hope you will not mind if I clear off this bench and take a seat. I have had a long drive in this cold." The cunning corporal made a show of blowing on his hands to warm them. He'd left his gloves behind in the Toyota—the better to handle his pistol when the time came—and he hoped his bare hands wouldn't raise her suspicions. "It is nearly freezing out here and I wonder if I could trouble you for a cup of hot coffee."

"This isn't some roadside truck stop," Mrs. Liberstein scoffed. "So, say what you came to say, then turn the blessed hell around and get the hell off my property. I spotted you coming the second you entered my long driveway, and you should know that I've already called the sheriff and my neighbors, and reinforcements will be here any minute."

Hearing this declaration, Karl glanced furtively at the Liberstein house, seeking to verify the notion which had struck him the moment he'd driven into the farmyard. His hurried glimpse confirmed what he'd suspected, which was that no telephone wires led to the Liberstein farmhouse. And this old woman didn't strike him as a member of the cellphone generation.

So, the corporal told himself, *no one is coming.*

"Very well," said Karl as he side-stepped past the water well until he reached the base of a huge tree which dominated the otherwise featureless farmyard. "I am not coming nearer," he explained. "I am merely moving sideways to sit." Stopping beneath the tree, he leaned down to brush a layer of snow off the wooden bench which pressed against the trunk. He sat down beneath the bare branches, blew on his hands once more, and casually loosened his heavy coat leaving only the two highest buttons fastened. "Allow me to introduce myself. You will know me as Rumpelstiltskin, and I am here about the nickels."

"*Fass!*" Mrs. Liberstein instantly commanded the dog and Karl had only seconds to reach inside his coat and level the pistol at the charging animal. He slowed the dog with his first shot, but the powerful beast latched onto his forearm and took a painful bite before it fell away. And, because Mrs. Liberstein had hesitated to shoot—probably for fear of hitting the dog—the nimble corporal was still able to pump two shots into the unlucky woman before she could fire either barrel of her useless shotgun.

Clearing the scene, Karl picked up the shotgun, pulled the woman's limp body inside, and deposited her unceremoniously on the living room floor. There was a time for leaving breadcrumbs and a time for discretion. Hansel and Gretel was a fairy tale he recalled from childhood, but it was only a story. Unlike the lost children in that nursery fable,

Karl had no desire to be discovered. He wanted to be noticed, not found. He was nearing the climax of his mission and he needed to be more judicious about scattering clues around Delta County. Better if this troublesome woman's body was not discovered just yet. He didn't bother to check for a pulse—that bit of dramatic fluff was the stuff of cinema and television. The efficient corporal was sure of his shots. No need and no time to second-guess himself.

Although his arm ached from the dog's savage attack, he made a rapid search of the ground floor, ignoring the kitchen and bathroom—hoping all the while that he wouldn't have to climb the stairs. Within moments, he determined that a large potted plant had been moved to one side wrinkling the living room's otherwise horizontal area rug.

Once a prisoner, always a prisoner, the corporal told himself as he marveled at the predictable tendency of concentration camp survivors to hide things beneath floorboards.

Peeling the rug up to reveal the wooden floor beneath, Karl knelt and used the butt of his pistol to tap the slats. Detecting loose and hollow-ringing boards, he pried them up and retrieved a three-ring notebook. A cursory study confirmed that the document was a photocopy of Herbert's Schulz's illusive manuscript. Unfortunately, the copy was incomplete.

The partial manuscript which the resourceful corporal had stolen from the sheriff's evidence locker had consisted of a few intact chapters. This new notebook covered more ground, but it presented its own problems because every other page was missing. Caroline née Gerda had only even pages which probably meant her wartime colleague possessed the odd ones. Karl's next stop would be the church in Delta City where the refugee Wolfgang Kjolhede was masquerading as a man of the cloth.

Back outside, Karl tore a strip from his shirttail and wrapped it tightly around his bleeding forearm. Then he cursed and gave the dead dog a violent kick before carrying the animal a few feet and pitching the carcass into the well.

After disposing of the dog, the corporal moved the Tacoma closer to the barn, hefted the diminutive Tiff out of the backseat, and carried the still-groggy woman inside. He lugged her to an empty stall, placed her in a corner, and—after checking her bonds—molded her into a fetal position, covered her with a blanket, and buried her form under a layer of loose hay.

Thus, he told himself, *another breadcrumb is strategically hidden. This fragile woman may not survive the cold, but we shall let fate decide.*

Without a further thought of Tiff, Karl conducted a search of the barn and other outbuildings. It was a rapid yet thorough inspection which yielded negative results. If the war nickels were here, they were well hidden.

And yet, their absence reinforced another, more likely scenario which Karl had come to embrace. Everything seemed to point in the same direction. The corporal reviewed the plausible explanation in his mind:

The moment Herbert Schulz's death became general knowledge, the conspirators would have moved the treasure trove of nickels to a safer place. I have come here intending to question Caroline Liberstein before killing her, but that is now impossible. I must move on to the next resource.

"Now for the priest," Karl said aloud not bothering to give Father Thomas his correct Protestant designation. He should have started with the old sinner first, but he'd soon rectify that misstep. "It is time to muddy the fount," he said as he started the Tacoma.

Chapter 27

Santa Claus
(January 1 / 10:30 a.m.)

Texas Ranger Emeritus Dallas ("Fingers") Heckleson stifled a sneeze. Leaping into the frozen clutches of the Gunnison River around midnight had not been one of his better ideas. It would be just his luck if this morning's early misadventure caused him to catch a bad cold. He repositioned the blanket to cover his bare feet and leaned closer to absorb the warmth of his roaring fireplace.

His friend, the detective, had driven him from Delta City and through the 'dobies to deposit him at his two-story stone house. After helping his comrade inside, Trinidad Sands had left the old ranger on his own to get out of his wet clothes. Thank God for small favors. It was bad enough to be rescued from an icy river and be escorted home like a delinquent teenager. The old ranger couldn't have stomached the ignominy of being undressed by a younger man and sent to bed without his supper.

Thinking of supper, Heckleson sighed.

"I need soup," he declared. "The hotter the better."

After rapidly feeding himself, the old ranger decided to get dressed and head to Cedaredge. One cure for his lingering depression, he reasoned, might be to return to the nearby town in order to revisit the scene of his recent holiday triumph. As he donned his jacket, he glanced in the mirror. He'd let his hair grow long and allowed his pure white beard to reach Biblical proportions—all in order to feel authentic when recently playing the part of the season's community Santa Claus. The kids had adored him—the ladies too. From Thanksgiving until Christmas Eve, he'd held forth every Saturday at the Grand Mesa Arts & Events Center, devoting his time and his ample lap to scores of wide-eyed youngsters. For the old recluse who'd been spending far too much time alone, those weekend performances had been nothing short of heavenly.

"You're the best Santa we've ever had," Caroline Liberstein had declared, and Herbert Schulz had agreed. Now Herbert was dead, and Caroline had retreated to her farm, either angry or grieving, or both, and Heckleson had never felt more alone. Since retiring from his Santa role in late December, he'd been at loose ends.

He'd interacted with Trinidad and Annie Sands of course, and Sheriff Jack Treadway had been a periodic contact. But those interactions simply weren't the same as communing with people from his own generation. And the population of those with shared memories was steadily dwindling. Moreover, neither the detective nor the sheriff had asked the old ranger to help with the current investigation into Herbert's untimely death. This slight may have been unintentional, but it added to Heckleson's depression. Life was passing the retired lawman by—like a runaway train hustling along a one-way track—traveling too fast for him to climb on board and bound for somewhere he couldn't follow.

Caught up in a cycle of morose thoughts, Heckleson stared hard at his reflection. Then he grabbed his rifle from its resting place in the kitchen corner and headed out.

The old ranger's stone house sat high atop a stark brown hill in the very heart of the bleak landscape which the locals called the 'dobies. It was an isolated spot, devoid of trees and traffic, which—at one time—had suited him just fine. Now the isolation merely made him sad.

After locking his back door, Heckleson shuffled across his broad rear porch and cautiously descended a steep exterior staircase. He paused halfway down to consider the view. Wispy clouds floated in the clear blue sky—a sharp contrast to the dusky purple outline of the lofty Grand Mesa. Last night's intermittent snow flurries had dusted the 'dobies with a patina of white which gave the nearby brown-dirt landscape the appearance of an undulating expanse of sugared gingerbread. The distant Grand Mesa also sported a mantle of white. It was a glorious view and Heckleson took several moments to take it all in.

At last, he descended the remaining stairsteps, walked to his vehicle, and climbed onboard. Firing up his vintage Chevy pickup, Heckleson carefully drove down his sharply sloping entry road and onto a narrow unpaved path which meandered through the 'dobies. His tires picked up muck and pebbles as he traversed the muddy stretch to reach a slightly wider ribbon of asphalt which would, in turn, connect to Highway 65. As he drove, the old ranger sighed, realizing he'd have to stop by the Lavender car wash and give the pickup's undercarriage a good going over before the mud hardened.

At the highway intersection, he yielded the right-of-way to a dark Toyota Tacoma. With a practiced eye, the old ranger noted that the vehicle's headlight was damaged—the result no doubt of a collision. Also, the lower portion of its dull finish was coated in a patina of wet mud—indicating that, like his own truck, the vehicle had recently traveled on an unpaved surface. As the speeding Toyota approached, the driver slowed down and took a long hard look at the ranger and his pickup.

Heckleson nodded in the direction of the passing motorist. He didn't recognize the vehicle, but rural etiquette dictated that, at minimum, he nod and raise an index finger in general acknowledgement. When he did so, the Toyota braked abruptly and sat idling just beyond the intersection.

For a heartbeat, the vehicle's back-up lights flickered then, just as suddenly, those lights disengaged, and the Toyota sped away.

"There's a lad who don't seem to know if he's comin' or goin' in this world," the old ranger told himself. "And my guess is he couldn't organize a bun fight in a bakery. Anyway, looks like him and me is both on the road to Lavender."

Heckleson turned toward the village and followed the Toyota at a distance. Seconds later, some sixth sense compelled the old ranger to shift into law enforcement mode. With one hand on the steering wheel, he reached into his pocket, fished out an envelope and a pencil, and made a note of the Toyota's Arizona license number.

"You never know," he told himself.

Up ahead, Karl Bistro glanced in his rearview mirror. He'd remember the old truck with its Texas license plate, and he'd also remember the isolated intersection. Moreover, he'd most certainly remember the occupant. The loyal corporal had been dispatched to Western Colorado to do his duty and it seemed perfectly logical that his efforts, which were so vital to the cause, would be closely monitored by his superior.

Seeing a bearded person who so closely resembled Santa Claus might be coincidental. Karl would know soon enough. If this same person followed him or appeared a second time, Karl's emerging impression would be confirmed. He drove on, pursuing his mission while also contemplating the authentic possibility that, for the very first time, he'd been graced with a glimpse of his past, present, and future—all united in a single person.

For, as improbable as it seemed, he had to seriously consider the possibility that he'd just laid eyes on his master.

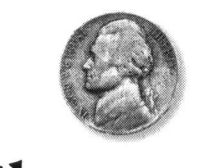

Chapter 28

Rumpelstiltskin
(January 1 / 11:00 a.m.)

After leaving Liberstein Farm and encountering a Santa Claus look-alike, Corporal Karl Bistro kept an eye on his rearview mirror as he steered his Toyota Tacoma through the Village of Lavender on his way toward Delta City. As a result, Karl was watching closely when the truck behind him left the highway.

Unaware of being scrutinized, Texas Ranger Emeritus Dallas Heckleson made a sharp right turn in order to visit Lavender's Jiffy-Spiffy Carwash, thus breaking off his informal pursuit of the Toyota. When Karl saw the old Chevy pickup leave the pavement, he was both relieved and disappointed.

"Perhaps we will meet again," the corporal told himself.

Two seconds later, Karl's cellphone pinged with a message from his master, the contents of which made it abundantly clear that the sender was nowhere near Western Colorado. Angered by what he perceived as a false masquerade perpetrated by the driver of the old pickup, Karl made an abrupt U-turn and found a secluded spot with a view of the car wash. As the imposter stood forty yards away, directing a high-powered spray onto the muddy undercarriage of his truck, Karl pulled his JS-2 rifle from its case and steadied his aim.

"Yet another distant encounter," he told himself aloud. "Ah well," he sighed. "Cannot be avoided," he assured himself.

His first shot knocked the would-be Santa off his feet. Just to make certain of his kill, Karl put one more round into the prostrate form. Then he replaced his rifle and resumed his original errand. Snow was beginning to fall and given the season, it would probably be some time before anyone using the car wash would discover the body. Like Schulz on the ice, he'd leave the pretender where he fell.

"A fitting end," the corporal told himself aloud, "for such a brazen imposter."

Thirty minutes later, when Karl reached Delta City, he made certain his actions were unobserved as he tucked an envelope under the windshield wiper of an unoccupied patrol car. His timing was ideal. The officer was busy sorting out a fender-bender and the eyes of other onlookers were on the accident. If this portion of Karl's scheme worked, the contents of the envelope would send the law on a nine-mile wild goose hunt. While the sheriff chased his tail, Karl himself would be paying a courtesy-call at the city's Episcopal sanctuary.

Moments later, it was snowing hard when Lieutenant Madge Oxford returned to her patrol car, discovered the envelope, and immediately headed for the station.

"Got something," Madge radioed the dispatcher. "I'm heading in. Have the boss meet me pronto."

Madge and Sheriff Jack Treadway were alone in the station's forensic lab. Jack had assigned Deputies Nichols and Phillips to pursue leads in the Schulz murder while he and Madge dealt with this latest crisis. The moment Madge brought him the evidence, he'd sworn his faithful lieutenant to secrecy, and she hadn't hesitated.

"No worries, Boss. Just tell me what you need me to do," the lieutenant said.

Jack stared at the newly-discovered ransom note then handed the sheet back to his lieutenant. Both officers were wearing disposable examination gloves. Madge had donned hers when she found the envelope. Jack had gloved up after the lieutenant arrived.

"What do you make of that signature?" the sheriff asked with anxiety evident in his voice. He was thankful that

Madge had agreed to help because he was far too close to the situation to function rationally.

"Rumpelstiltskin? From the fairy tale, I guess," Madge responded as she studied the odd name. "You're certain it's not Tiff's handwriting?"

Jack raised an eyebrow. "Don't even go there," he growled.

"Just saying—" Madge began.

"Don't—" he warned.

"Okay," Madge relented. "So, we're assuming it's a legit ransom note. What now?"

Jack was silent for a moment. His head was throbbing from last night's binge and this afternoon's shock of learning that Tiff may be in danger had further confounded him. When at last he spoke, it was in a voice taut with emotion, "We follow procedure."

"Check," said Madge.

Jack crossed the room and killed the overhead light. Madge used her gloved fingers to flatten the note into an examination frame. Then, while Jack joined her at the waist-high light table, Madge centered the frame and toggled the table switch to the on position. The incandescent bulbs flickered to life making the frosted glass glow like a luminous sheet of phosphorescent ice and bathing the two officers in an eerie glow of greenish light.

"No return address on the envelope," said Madge, glancing at her Smartphone to make certain her observations were being recorded. "The envelope is a standard number-ten, measuring 4 1/8 by 9 ½ inches. Envelope was discovered at 11:47 a.m. on January 1, 2020, positioned beneath driver's side windshield wiper of Lieutenant Margaret Oxford's patrol car. Contents are a standard trifold of a single sheet of 8 ½ by 11 inch white bond paper—no watermark—no masthead. Smudges in upper right- and left-hand corners of the fold and small circular textured indentations in both locations suggest paper, before and after folding, was handled by someone wearing rubber gloves. Size of hypothetical thumb indentation suggests handler was male. No saliva DNA on the envelope seal—residue suggests sender used a sponge to wet the glue. No prints on the envelope or the contents—confirming theory that sender wore gloves. Note is handwritten—

"Which suggests," Jack interrupted, "that the sender was confident that his or her handwritin' wouldn't be familiar to recipients. Letters are legible, but somewhat distorted, which again suggests sender wore gloves while writin'. No words obviously misspelled nor grammar mistakes."

"So," Madge concluded, "this isn't your typical ransom note. No cut-and-paste of clipped-out letters from newspapers. No spelling errors or grammar missteps designed to try convincing us that the writer is less than literate. Not much to go on."

Madge turned off the recorder and the two stared at the note—examining it for perhaps the tenth time. Then Jack motioned for his lieutenant to turn the recorder back on as he read the note aloud, this time for the record:

"Message reads: 'Sheriff, your girlfriend is my prisoner. *Her life for all the nickels.* (Underlined) Bring them all and come alone to the intersection of Harts Basin and North Road. No tricks or she dies. You have until 1 p.m. today to comply. (Signed) Rumpelstiltskin.'"

"*All the nickels?*" Madge turned off the recorder and repeated the question which had been plaguing both officers. "What the heck is that supposed to mean?"

"I wish the hell I knew," Jack sighed as once again he sought to rack his brain. The words seemed to remind him of something—maybe something he'd read. He tried to recall the meaning, but his efforts were in vain. His hangover from last night's booze seemed to block his thinking, or it might be a fog of irrational guilt over his failure to protect a woman whom—despite her faults—he still adored. Whatever clouded his memory, his mind was buzzing and, try as he might, he just couldn't remember. His thoughts were interrupted by a knock on the forensic lab's door.

"They said not to interrupt," the officer apologized when Jack opened the door. "But I need your signature before we transfer the Denver prisoner to booking."

Jack stood in the doorway with the knob in his gloved hand. He was staring past the man's shoulder and seemed not to hear.

Sergeant Harold Drake was a patient man, a common trait among K9 handlers. The enterprising sergeant had finagled a temporary transfer from the Carbondale police to Jack's crew by convincing both Jack and his Carbondale boss that the Delta County Sheriff's office needed to experience the advantages of having a working dog on call. That was the "official" reason for Drake's short-term transfer. The real reason was that Drake wanted to spend some time in Delta City in order to have an excuse to run into the lovely Annie Scriptor with whom, having seen her exactly twice, he'd fallen madly in love.

He'd first encountered Annie at a roadblock on McClure Pass and then again at the Carbondale Library standoff when his K9 companion, Cozy, had rescued the courageous woman. And both times she'd struck him as spunky and brave and absolutely adorable. When Cozy was shot in the line of duty and Annie adopted the injured dog, Drake sensed an opportunity. Selling himself and his new K9 as a package deal, he crossed his fingers and requested a transfer.

Arriving in Delta City to begin his interim assignment, Drake was a bit crestfallen to be invited to a celebration where he learned that the vivacious Miss Scriptor was now Mrs. Trinidad Sands. But his momentarily broken heart soon mended when his attention was drawn to a redhead who worked at the hardware store. Drake prided himself that—where love was concerned—he was nothing if not flexible.

"Um," Drake cleared his throat, indicated the transfer paperwork, and reminded Jack that it was his turn to act. "Sheriff, it's your nickel—"

Seeming to awaken from a stupor, Jack suddenly recalled the significance of the word *nickel*. The sheriff snatched the form and scribbled his signature. "Give this paperwork to the front desk," he ordered. "Then grab your weapon and meet me at the parking lot."

"Yes, sir," said Drake as he moved quickly down the corridor.

"And Drake—" Jack called after the officer.

"Sheriff—?" The sergeant stopped in the corridor waiting for Jack to finish his thought.

"Bring your dog!" Jack shouted as he sprinted toward his office, intent on retrieving the binder containing samples from old man Schulz's unpublished autobiography.

Over a year ago, Herbert had stopped Jack on a Lavender sidewalk and handed the sheriff a ring-bound notebook containing four rudimentary chapters.

"I know you like a good mystery," Herbert told Jack.

"The War Nickel," Jack observed as he examined the title page. "So, it's about WWII, I reckon."

"Bingo," said Herbert. Then he leaned forward and whispered conspiratorially. "All about the War and those contemptible Nazis. And now," Herbert winked, "here's a little something for your trouble." The old man handed Jack two seemingly ordinary nickels. "Consider these two five-cent pieces an advance payment in anticipation of you giving me your two-cents worth of feedback on my writing."

A keen town observer may have seen Herbert slip the notebook and the coins to Jack, or perhaps a network of local gossipers had picked up other clues. Whatever caused the stir, soon everyone in Lavender seemed to know that Herbert was writing a book and the question most often asked of the sheriff was a predictable, "Am I in it?"

"Not unless you were of draft age in the 1940s," Jack answered.

"Oh," was the invariable reply.

When word got around that Herbert's writing concerned neither Lavender nor the village citizenry, local curiosity waned. Even Jack, who'd started reading the sample chapters with best intentions, began to lose interest. The binder had been added to a stack on his cluttered desk. Months passed and Jack came within a whisker of spilling coffee on it.

Chagrined at his carelessness, the sheriff made a photocopy, placed the original in the station's evidence locker, and began reading the copy. But he stopped when Tiff came into his life and commenced—in her seductive way—to monopolize his spare time.

Now Jack recognized where he'd read about the nickels—*the war nickels*—and he congratulated himself for adding a potential missing piece to the puzzle of Herbert Schulz's murder and possibly rediscovering a key to comprehending the chaos which had subsequently infected Delta County.

Chapter 29

A Nickel for Your Thoughts
(January 1 / Noon)

It was snowing hard when Madge Oxford's call came through on the landline. Trinidad was out in the driveway, piloting the farm's reliable all-terrain vehicle as he plowed a path through the drifting snow. Taking the call, Annie stepped out on the front porch and waggled the receiver in her husband's direction.

"It's Madge!" she shouted over the din of the ATV. "It sounds urgent!"

"Be there in a jiffy," Trinidad yelled back and, true to his word, he wheeled the vehicle toward the porch, parked it neatly, throttled down, and killed the engine.

"I don't think you're making any headway in this storm," she said, studying the swirling snow and leaden sky, as she handed him the phone.

"Just an excuse to be outside," he said with a grin as he pushed his hood back and removed his mittens. "Duffy's Tavern—Duffy ain't here—" he began with a joke but immediately grew somber as he listened intently. "Sorry—yes—of course—we're on our way—wait repeat that—did you say *nickels*?"

Trinidad left the ATV where it had landed, and he sent Annie inside to grab his rifle and her pistol and bundle up. Then he rushed to the garage to fire up the Ridgeline. It only took Annie a moment to secure weapons and ammunition, then don her cold-weather gear and join him in the front cab.

"Where to?" she asked as Trinidad maneuvered the Ridgeline through the farmyard and started uphill toward the dormant lavender fields. "And why?"

"Jack's been reading his copy of the Schulz manuscript and he's convinced almost everyone we know is in danger. I'm headed to join Madge at Father Thomas' church," he said when the Ridgeline reached the flat and gathered speed. "Tiff's missing. Jack's in Eckert. And Madge thinks Mrs. Liberstein may be in harm's way, so I'm supposed to drop you at her place."

"What kind of danger? And which nickels?" she asked, recalling one side of Trinidad's phone conversation with Madge.

"No firm idea on the danger," said Trinidad as he reached the county road and skidded onto the snowbound pavement.

"Except to say there's a rogue shooter loose in the county. And having read Herb's manuscript, you and I know as much about nickels as anybody hereabouts. Excepting maybe Jack, Fingers Heckleson, and probably Caroline Liberstein."

"Here's another fine mess," said Annie.

"I know this one," said Trinidad. "W.C. Fields, right?"

"Close," Annie said and despite the tension of their mysterious assignments she managed a chuckle. "It's Laurel and Hardy— Slow down, we need to turn here. Hey! What the heck?"

Trinidad stopped at the top of the Liberstein road as he and Annie examined the downed mailbox and the tire marks etched into the snowbank at the base of the severed pole.

"Somebody missed their turn," said Annie.

"Somebody new to these parts who didn't know where they were going," Trinidad decided as he studied the skid marks. "Went past going fast and tried to turn after they were beyond her road. I'll prop up the box on the way out. Let's get you down to Caroline's." Trinidad steered the Honda onto the Liberstein road and into an already existing set of tracks. "We ain't the first," he observed. "Looks like her reckless visitor's come and gone already."

"Tell you what," said Annie, "at the next rise we can see all the way to the farmhouse and if there's no strange vehicles down there, let me off there and I'll walk down the rest of the way."

"You sure?" he asked.

"Yes," she insisted. "Jack needs you to go to Delta City, so no sense wasting time. I'll be okay," she said while also making certain her holstered pistol was firmly belted around her waist.

"This is a bad start," said Trinidad. Since co-founding the newly formed Sands Detective Agency, he and his bride had pledged to do their detecting as an inseparable team.

"I know," she sympathized. "Already we're breaking our New Year's resolution not to be separated on a case, but that can't be helped today."

"Call or text me right away when you're safely inside," he said. "Promise."

"Promise," she said as the Ridgeline came to a stop. She released her seatbelt, got out, and stood clear to watch while Trinidad expertly maneuvered the Honda to-and-fro to turn around.

The novice detective told herself that she was lingering there just to make certain her husband didn't get stuck in the ditches. But she also felt compelled to get a final glimpse of him.

Just in case, she told herself and, aloud, she shouted, "Stay safe!"

"You too!" he responded as he motored back to the county road.

Annie watched him go. Then she turned and trudged the half-mile downhill to the Liberstein farm. She was wading through the ever-deepening snow and nearing the front porch when she saw the blood.

Chapter 30

Music

(January 1 / 12:15 p.m.)

Ducking behind the broad farmyard tree for cover, Annie Sands drew her weapon.

"Police!" she lied. "Let's see your hands!

When she heard nothing but the winter wind and the creaking of the weathervane high on the crest of the Liberstein barn, she added, "I've got a gun!"

Peeking around the tree trunk she saw a nearly straight line of blood leading across the farmyard snow. The bright red line began near the front porch and terminated at the water well. Fearing the worst, Annie sidled to the edge of the well and looked down.

"Oh no," she said. "Music, you poor kid."

What had possessed Caroline Liberstein to give her vicious Rottweiler such a pitiful name was anybody's guess, but Annie could see that Music was a goner.

"Hello!" Annie turned and shouted in the direction of the house. "Caroline? Mrs. Liberstein, can you hear me?"

A barely perceptible moan emanated from the house and the brave young woman threw caution to the wind as she raced up the front steps following yet another trail of blood. "I'm coming in!" Annie shouted. "And I'm armed!" And with that final warning, the fledgling detective shouldered her way into the farmhouse and began scanning the dwelling, sidling through doorways and aiming her pistol at exaggerated angles as she sought to mirror the deliberate law enforcement actions which she'd seen in movies and on television.

"I said, I'm armed!" Annie yelled again as she approached the living room.

"My goodness, girl," said Mrs. Liberstein. "I heard you the first time. Give us a hand, love."

Annie rushed through the doorway and found Caroline lying on her side in a pool of blood.

"What happened—?" Annie began as she holstered her weapon and knelt beside the stricken woman.

"Worthless Nazi," Caroline coughed. "Two shots and he only winged me. No wonder they lost the war."

"Can you sit up?" Annie asked. "*Should* you sit up? Where are you hit?"

"Heavens," Caroline scolded, "have you never seen someone shot before?"

Annie had to admit it was her first time.

"Well, don't fret, child," the older woman assured her. "I've had worse than this and lived. Just grazed my head and a thru-and-thru in the shoulder. My bulked-up parka absorbed most of the lead. Those two shots just knocked me out mostly. Fortunately, the careless villain was in a rush and didn't check my pulse. Wonder why he was in such a hurry —oh damn!" Caroline exclaimed as she noticed the crumpled rug and pile of floor slats.

"Pain?" Annie asked.

"No!" Caroline cried. "Not a pain-damn! Another kind of damn entirely! Do you have your fancy phone with you? Good! So, I pray to God that, between the two of us, we will remember the phone number of the Delta City Episcopal Church!"

Chapter 31

A Pastoral Visit
(January 1 / 12:30 p.m.)

    Simultaneous actions were unfolding at diverse Western Colorado locations. Sheriff Jack Treadway drove alone toward the remote spot described in the ransom note, with lights flashing but no siren. Sergeant Harold Drake backed up the sheriff by racing to set up a Highway 65 checkpoint. From the Sheriff's office, Lieutenant Madge Oxford rushed to the nearby Delta City Episcopal Church. Detective Trinidad Sands sped from the Village of Lavender toward that same church, while Caroline Liberstein and Annie Sands huddled in the Liberstein living room as they searched for the church's phone number. Meanwhile, Father Thomas stood in the rectory hallway, fingering an envelope as he studied the painting hanging there.

    Father Thomas loved that painting.

He'd adored it since the first time he saw it as a newly arrived immigrant, on display in Washington, D.C.'s National Gallery. The rectory image was a print of course, but a faithful reproduction of Richard Norris Brooke's 1881 oil painting depicting a Black preacher sitting at a rural table while a family of five—a mother and father and three children—assembled nearby. Oh, how Father Thomas longed to inspire the rapt attention exhibited by almost every member of that righteous family.

"Everyone pictured here is attending closely to the preacher. Except you, my pet," he said aloud as he tapped the glazing which separated his stubby fingers from the framed print. His focus was on the youngest child whose face was buried in her father's knee. "You are not paying attention," he chided. "So, I fear for your soul, little one. I truly do."

"A masterpiece," said a voice behind him.

Father Thomas hadn't heard the stranger enter, nor had he felt a rush of cold air. "Ah, my son," Thomas said, "you must have entered through the sanctuary, I surmise. How may I help you?"

"I am here," said Karl Bistro as he sidled into the room, easing the door shut behind him, "about the coins."

"You wish to make a donation?" the clergyman asked hopefully.

"Not today," Karl said. "I desire to make a withdrawal."

"I don't understand," said Father Thomas, and he adjusted his spectacles, possibly thinking that seeing more clearly would help him comprehend.

"Wolfgang Kjolhede," the unrepentant corporal intoned the colorful Danish name and was pleased to see that the effect of hearing it caused Thomas to pale. "This may or may not be your lucky day."

In shock, the befuddled clergyman yielded to the stranger's powerful grip and allowed his quaking body to be man-handled through the rectory door and into the cramped passageway which led behind the organ pipes. In the brief struggle, Father Thomas dropped the envelope he'd been holding, and the church's unpaid phone bill fluttered down to land on the hallway floor just as the rectory telephone began to ring.

Chapter 32

Text

(January 1 / 12:40 p.m.)

"No answer at the church," said Annie. "So, I'll text Trinidad. What should I say?"

"Danger!" said Caroline. "Help Thomas and call police!"

"Okay," said Annie. "But Lieutenant Oxford will probably beat my husband to the church, so the cops will surely already be there."

"Send it anyway," Caroline insisted, "and tell that husband of yours to warn the police as well. Assuming it isn't too late—" her voice trailed off and she felt faint.

"Text is on its way," said Annie. "Now it's 911 to get an ambulance rolling out here and pass on a warning to Madge."

As Annie made her call, Caroline, who was slumped on the living room sofa, stared up at the younger woman with a look of admiration. "We could have used you in '42," the old woman said before she swooned.

Chapter 33

Hart's Basin
(January 1 / 12:55 p.m.)

It had stopped snowing. Sheriff Jack Treadway sat at the junction of Hart's Basin and North Road. Setting the binder containing chapters of Herbert Schulz's manuscript aside, the sheriff rummaged through his glove compartment in search of a cigarette. At Tiff's insistence, he'd given up smoking.

"If I wanted to taste tobacco," she'd said after refusing to kiss him until he gave up his nicotine habit, "I'd lick an ashtray."

Motivated by love and lust, Jack had quit cold-turkey. Now, having checked his house and Tiff's workplace and confirmed that Tiff was missing, he needed a smoke.

"Dang," he said as he fished an empty pack out of the far corner of the compartment. An unexpected tap on his window startled him.

"Lost something?" Desmond Adams asked, and he stepped back as Jack rolled down the patrol car's window. The old wrangler was wearing a red and black checkered topcoat with his signature Stetson and a weathered scarf wrapped around his neck. His horse stood behind him, its head down and the breath from its nostrils blowing the powdery snow aside as it searched in vain for a morsel.

"On the job," said Jack. "So, I need you to move along, okay?"

"Okay," said Desmond as he turned to leave.

"Wait just a second," said Jack and he motioned the cowboy back. "How long have you been out here, and have you seen any vehicles on the road today?"

"Out here kicking the ice off the stock ponds since morning," said Desmond. "No cars in all that time."

"Thanks," said Jack. "Do me a favor?"

"Sure."

"Keep clear of down here but ride up on the bluff and have a look-see. Take this bandanna and wave it side-to-side if you see anythin' at all—any cars—any people—understand? I'll be able to spot you from down here. Side-to-side if you see anythin'—remember. And also, if it's all-clear, wave the bandanna up-and-down, savvy?"

"Okay," said Desmond. "You're the boss."

Jack watched as the expert rider mounted up and guided his sure-footed horse to the top of the bluff which overlooked the intersection. From that height, Desmond would have a clear view of the junction as well as Hart's Basin and Fruit Grower's Reservoir beyond. When Desmond reached the top, Jack stared intently and, seconds later, he saw the old wrangler waving the red bandanna continuously and unambiguously up-and-down.

"Aw hell!" Jack growled and he reached for the radio. He raised Sergeant Harold Drake whom he'd posted at the intersection of Highway 65 and North Road and assigned him to take his K9 to the Village of Lavender with orders to search the Liberstein farm.

"What are we looking for, Boss?" Drake asked.

"Whatever you find," said Jack. "I'm runnin' short of ideas."

The sheriff would wait another hour and, if there was no sign of the kidnapper, he'd hit the siren and head back to Delta City, cursing all the way.

Chapter 34

Search

(January 1 / 1:45 p.m.)

Sergeant Harold Drake found the Liberstein turnoff and started down the long, sloping driveway, inserting his patrol car into the well-worn track created by other vehicles. His fearless K9, Mitzie, had her ears on full alert as the clever dog sensed that she was about to go to work.

"Good girl," Drake cooed. "Almost there."

When he reached a curve, he met an ambulance coming up and was just able to get his patrol car far enough onto the narrow shoulder to allow the emergency vehicle to pass. As the ambulance drew abreast, Drake rolled down his window and the other driver did the same.

"What gives?" he asked the paramedic at the wheel.

"Transporting Caroline Liberstein to Delta County Emergency," he said. "Gunshot. She'll be okay. The girl detective is still down there."

"You mean Annie?"

"I guess," said the paramedic. "We wasn't exactly properly introduced. But she might of said a name like that. Gotta run."

"Copy that," said Drake as the ambulance moved on. He spoke to Mitzie while the two of them headed downhill toward the farmhouse in the distance. "That enticing gal keeps popping up," he told the alert dog. "Maybe it's *Kismet*."

The word caught Mitzie's attention and she inclined her head.

"Kismet," Drake repeated. "Fate—destiny—you know?"

Mitzie barked.

"Wishful thinking—you got that right, old girl," Drake said as he reached the bottom of the long driveway and steered across the farmyard toward the small two-story house which lay beyond. *Small house, big barn,* he smiled to himself. *Welcome to Lavender Village.*

Annie was standing on the front porch and, as Drake pulled to a stop, he was intrigued to see that the beautiful object of his unrequited affection was wearing a holster and pistol.

"Just me," the sergeant said as he emerged from his vehicle holding up one hand. "Don't shoot."

"Mitzie!" said Annie as she saw the enthusiastic dog leap from the patrol car and bolt past her master.

"Well," said Drake with a chuckle, "I'm at least impressed that you recognize my dog."

"Officer Smiley," Annie said, and she joined the sergeant in a chuckle as Mitzie greeted her and danced around the porch. "Not that I'm not pleased to see you too, but what brings you all the way out here?"

"I've been dispatched to search the place," Drake explained. "Though I ain't sure for what."

"Any chance Mitzie can sniff out a barrel of nickels?" Annie asked as she petted the affectionate dog.

"Pardon?"

"Never mind," said Annie. "I'll let you two get to work."

"Search, girl!" Drake commanded and Mitzie favored Annie with one final affectionate glance, then the reliable animal dashed into the house and went through her paces.

It didn't take long for the efficient dog to sniff her way through both floors of the compact farmhouse and, after a detour to study the blood stain on the living room rug, Mitzie bolted out of the house and made a beeline for the water well where she barked repeatedly until Drake came for a look. He leaned over the edge of the well and swept the bottom with his flashlight beam.

"That's Caroline's dog down there," Annie informed Drake as she joined the sergeant at the well.

"Dang," Drake said. "Somebody's gonna pay for this," he added with an angry frown. "Search, girl, let's find us a worthless canine-killer!"

Mitzie wheeled around and sprinted toward the barn with Drake and Annie on her heels as they traversed the snow-covered ground. The speedy dog had nearly reached the barn when the sergeant paused her run.

"Mitzie, stay!" Drake shouted and the dog skidded to a halt outside the barn. "Tire tracks here," he noted when they reached the spot. "And not our ambulance. This is a Michelin Defender tread and probably a Tacoma. Same tread-marks as on the road coming down."

"So, come and gone?" Annie speculated.

"Maybe," said Drake as he pulled his weapon and crossed his wrists pointing both the pistol and the flashlight toward the gaping barn door. "You stay here," he told Annie.

"Don't have to tell me twice," Annie obeyed.

"Mitzie! Search!" Drake shouted as he entered the barn, uncertain what he might find in the inky recesses of the sprawling structure. "Police!" the sergeant's commanding voice reached Annie's ears from inside the barn. "Stay where you are! Show me your hands!"

Mitzie began barking and then there was prolonged silence followed by an agonizing delay as Annie remained outside the barn fidgeting with the keeper on her holster.

"Mrs. Sands," Drake finally called from the dark interior. "I need your help in here!"

"Which way?" Annie asked as she hesitated at the door.

"Here," Drake answered as he aimed the flashlight beam in her direction. "Hold this," he said when she arrived.

Entering a dank stall, Annie took the light from Drake's outstretched hand and pointed it toward the corner of the narrow enclosure.

"My God!" Annie gulped as the beam fell on Tiff's bedraggled face. "Is she—"

"She's breathing," said Drake. "But just barely. We need to get her into the house. You lead and I'll follow."

Annie watched as Drake picked up the stricken woman. Then she led the way out of the barn and across the snow as the tall man followed with Tiff's limp body in his arms. Mitzie trotted beside her master, whimpering in what might have been a show of sympathy for the injured person whom the questing dog had discovered and extracted from the concealing hay.

Drake lay Tiff on the living room couch and tried as gently as possible to untie the semi-conscious woman. Tiff suddenly gasped for air, as if about to drown, and the alert sergeant just had time to turn her head to the side before the distressed woman vomited profusely.

"That's a good sign," he informed Annie who was just hanging up from calling for the evening's second ambulance and scrounging through the Liberstein's kitchen drawers. "And good for you—that's exactly what we need here," he said as Annie handed him a sharp boning knife.

Drake carefully cut the ropes away and put the knife safely aside as Annie began rubbing Tiff's arms and legs.

"She's ice cold and these ropes have cut deep," Annie said, her voice cracking with emotion. "Oh, Tiff, can you hear me, girl? Wake up!"

"Her circulation's probably shot and hypothermia's just around the corner," said Drake as he lifted Tiff's eyelids to examine her pupils. "Shock," he pronounced as he stood up. "Strip her down to her underwear—I'll start a hot bath and get back here on the double with a blanket."

As Drake rushed from the room, Annie began peeling Tiff's clothes off as the distraught woman opened her eyes, managed a hoarse scream, and, unaware that someone was trying to help, began pushing and clawing at her friend.

"Tiff! Tiff!" Annie shouted. "It's okay! It's me. You're okay! We're going to get you warm!"

Aware of Tiff's distress, Mitzie, who had been lying on the carpet a few feet away, sprang to her feet and nuzzled the flailing woman.

"Dog," said Tiff and she grew calmer as she wrapped her arms around the affectionate animal's neck. "Good dog."

"Yes, good dog, Mitzie—good dog," said Annie as she hurriedly finished undressing the supine woman. Tiff lay motionless and breathing raggedly as Mitzie moved away. The room grew quiet until Drake returned on a dead run, carrying a blanket and intent on conveying the ailing woman to the bathroom tub.

"Here we go," said Drake.

"No! No! No!" Tiff screamed at the sight of the hulking man and the frantic woman held both arms out to fend him off. Mitzie barked as Tiff gulped for air then fell back, exhausted, upon the couch.

"I'll do it," said Annie as she signaled for Drake to stand aside. Taking the blanket, she snugged it around Tiff. Then she leaned confidently forward, put both arms underneath the petite girl, and lifted her up like it was something she did every day.

"Good job," said Drake with a tone of unvarnished admiration. "I'll get the door."

Chapter 35

Alley
(January 1 / Afternoon)

Unaware that others were in the process of rescuing and reviving Tiff Northbridge, Lieutenant Madge Oxford stood in a Delta City alleyway examining an unfamiliar Toyota Tacoma. The dark gray vehicle was parked in the alleyway alongside the Episcopal Church, close to the wall, as if someone wanted to conceal it.

The alert lieutenant had noticed the suspicious vehicle as she turned off the main street and drove past the narrow alley to reach the church's front parking lot. Stopping near the main entry door, she'd found the broad expanse of adjacent snow-covered asphalt completely empty and devoid of tire tracks. So, she'd parked her patrol car, called in the Toyota's Arizona license plate, and gotten out to walk back for a closer look.

Why park in the alley when there are plenty of closer spots? A delivery? the lieutenant asked herself.

The sheriff had sent Madge downtown to keep an eye on Father Thomas and report anything at the church which seemed unusual. This Toyota might be benign, but it was definitely out of place. She put her hand on the hood—still warm.

"Are you clear for your return?" Her shoulder radio squawked the inquiry. It was the county dispatcher asking if the receiving officer was free to copy down the vehicle information she'd requested.

"23 at Saint Luke's—go ahead," Madge reported her location.

"Your 28 is Adam-King-Ocean-1228, registered to a Hans Brinker, 81600 Coal-Slide Canyon Road, Cedaredge. Arizona registration current. No outstanding warrants."

"Copy that," Madge said as she recorded the facts in her notebook. Buttoning the notebook into her shirt pocket, she knelt down to study the Toyota's front headlight and fender where the metal had collided with something. She pressed a finger into the deep scratches and came away with slivers of silver paint and a curl of wood.

Recent, she thought as she glanced at the church wall and then up and down the alley seeing all brick and city concrete but nothing silver or wooden in view.

"Dispatch," Madge stood up and spoke into her microphone.

"Go ahead."

"Any hit-and-runs reported, Sharon?"

"Negative. Meantime, got a 911 message to pass on—Annie Sands says *be careful.*"

"Copy that. I'll be in church."

"About time," Sharon said with a laugh.

Madge tried the alley door, found it unlocked, and entered into a darkened hallway. She was just turning back to pull the door closed when a blow to the back of her neck sent her sprawling to the linoleum.

The lieutenant remembered nothing until Trinidad's voice broke through the fog in her brain.

"Madge? Madge? Can you hear me?" Trinidad asked.

"Tum-phhhota," the lieutenant managed to mumble.

"The paramedics are near," said Trinidad.

"Tuh-phum-ota," Madge mumbled.

"Okay," said Trinidad. "Here they come. Hear the siren?"

"Toyota," Madge finally managed to form the word.

"I understand," said Trinidad, although he wasn't sure what she meant. A heartbeat later, he heard voices at the front entrance as the ambulance crew arrived. "Down here!" he shouted.

Chapter 36

Brimstone
(January 1 / Afternoon)

The paramedics had Lieutenant Madge Oxford sitting on the hard linoleum floor with her back against the wall as they checked her vitals.

"Shine that light in my eye one more time, Bobby—" Madge began to voice a thinly-veiled threat.

"You're kidding right?" Bobby asked.

"I don't think she's kidding," said his partner, Andrew.

"Pretty sure she isn't kidding," observed Trinidad.

"Just making sure your pupils constrict," said Bobby. "You know the drill, Ox—I mean Lieutenant. Just making sure your brain works."

"Lots of blood where the skin was broken," said Andrew as he began to expertly bandage the back of Madge's neck. "The cut's not too bad, but this is one hell of a knot. Did you at least get the number of the truck that hit you?"

"As a matter of fact," said Madge, wincing as Andrew secured the dressing. "If the Toyota in the alley with the dented fender and cracked headlight is gone, I've not only got the number but also the name and address of the buzzard who bushwhacked me. And, if you two angels of mercy are done fussing around like mother hens on crack cocaine, I'll get back to work."

"No sign of Father Thomas?" Trinidad asked as he and Madge stood on the church steps watching the paramedics pack up.

"Didn't have a chance to look," said Madge.

"I get that," said Trinidad. "Anyway, I searched high and low while the paramedics were checking you out. The lights are on in his office and his tea pot was nearly boiled dry, but the rest of the church is totally dark and completely empty."

"Toyota took him probably," said Madge.

"Got ourselves another kidnapping?" Trinidad asked.

"Looks like," the lieutenant confirmed.

"Related?" the detective wondered.

"Probably," Madge observed.

"Now, about this dent in the Toyota—" Trinidad began, but his inquiry was interrupted by a ping on his cellphone. "Why does it do that? Here's a text from Annie which was sent more than twenty minutes ago. And the one I sent her earlier is still spinning in my out-box!"

"Western Colorado cellphone wasteland," Madge said.

"Hell's bells," Trinidad exclaimed as he examined Annie's text. "Caroline Liberstein's been shot, and Tiff is hurt."

"Tiff and Caroline both?"

"Yes, but they're both okay," Trinidad continued reading Annie's text. "Caroline says somebody needs to warn Father Thomas—too late for that. She also says somebody should check-out the old Schulz place. Caroline says her shooter was a stranger driving a primer-gray—"

"Toyota Tacoma," Madge and Trinidad said simultaneously.

"Gotta be the same vehicle I glimpsed in the snow at Island Lake and earlier in the pancake house parking lot," Trinidad remembered at last.

"Same busy buzzard, apparently," Madge decided.

"Madge, what's your *20?*" Her shoulder radio broadcasted the sheriff's voice.

Everything seemed to be happening at once.

"*10-23*, Saint Luke's. Do you copy?" said Madge.

"Copy. No-show here at Hart's Basin," said Jack. "And Drake radioed to say he's at the Liberstein place looking after—after—Tiff—"

As the sheriff's voice faltered, Madge picked up the slack.

"Doc Northbridge and the widow Liberstein are both okay I hear," Madge assured him.

Jack cursed aloud and immediately regretted using profanity on the radio. "Sorry—where do you think should I go?" His voice suggested that he was absolutely bewildered.

"We've got a line on the shooter," said Madge. "I'll take over. You go to Liberstein's."

"Copy," said Jack, the relief evident in his voice.

"Sharon, raise *4-7-1*," Madge said as she gave the dispatcher Sergeant Drake's call numbers.

"Copy," said Sharon. "*4-7-1*, what's your *20*?"

"Drake, *10-23*, Liberstein Farm," the sergeant responded.

Listening to this rapid-fire radio chatter, Trinidad guessed that a lay person would be getting lost about now. Luckily, he knew enough law enforcement code to recognize that *20* and *10-23* were location confirmation codes. *What's your 20?* means *What's your location?* and *10-23* is another way of saying *My location is—*.

"Oxford, *10-23*, Saint Luke's," Madge shoe-horned into the conversation. "Jack's on his way to you. I need you elsewhere and Detective Sands wants Annie."

"Copy that," said Drake with an unexpected burst of enthusiasm.

"Can paramedics stay with Doc until Jack gets there?" Madge asked.

After a pause Drake responded, "Affirmative. They aren't anxious to move her until she's more stable."

"I need you to drop Annie at the Lavender post office," Madge told Drake. "Sands will pick her up there. Then I need you to head up to Brimstone Corner and block the road. Sending backup now to help you evacuate civilians as needed and lock down Coal-Slide Canyon. I'll meet you up there soonest."

"What am I looking for at Brimstone?" Drake wondered.

"Sharon?" Madge inquired.

"I copy you both," the dispatcher responded. "I can fill Drake in, but where's Jack?"

"Sheriff's on his way—to perform—victim assistance." Madge decided to gloss over the details of what she anticipated would be an emotional reunion at Liberstein farm between Jack and Tiff. "Give *4-7-1* the vehicle description and suspect name and send backup out to Brimstone. All units to consider suspect armed and dangerous. And, Sharon, we'll need a warrant—names and address to follow. I'll be over to pick it up."

"Roger that," Sharon confirmed.

Madge's radio continued to squawk as Sharon relayed the lieutenant's orders.

"One of our hunches is liable to pan out," Madge told Trinidad before the two of them parted company to return to their respective vehicles. "I'm guessing the action will go down on Brimstone and you think the old Schulz place in Lavender is likely. Best if we divide and conquer. While you and Annie check-out the Schulz house, I'll send units to the village to back you up —just in case."

"Just in case," Trinidad agreed as he started his Honda. He was about to drive away when Madge pulled up beside him and honked. Her driver's side window was already down and, when Trinidad followed suit, she reached across and handed him a red and blue LED dashboard light.

"Don't make me regret this," she cautioned. "It plugs into the cigarette lighter. And keep the unit in one piece because I'm signed out for it. So, treat it gently."

"Like it was my very own special flasher," said Trinidad with a playful grin.

"Smart ass," said the lieutenant as she hit her siren and lights and wheeled into the street.

Tiff had been mostly incoherent, but she was temporarily lucid enough to describe her ordeal at Karl Bistro's manor. After dropping Annie at the Lavender Village post office, Sergeant Drake passed on Tiff's testimony and drove to Brimstone Corner. Reaching the spot, he parked and waited for backup to arrive. When a fresh crop of deputies appeared, two officers secured the intersection while four others dispersed to conduct a door-to-door mission to evacuate area civilians.

Fifteen minutes later, Lieutenant Oxford reached Brimstone and—thanks to Tiff's recollections—she brought a warrant with authorization to search the premises of *both* Hans Brinker *and* Karl Bistro.

"One name or the other is an alias," she informed Drake. "And my money's on the Brinker moniker. With me," she told the sergeant.

"Dog too?" he asked.

"Dog too," Madge confirmed.

With Drake and Mitzie onboard, Madge drove to the manor and concealed her patrol car at the base of the building's lengthy driveway. The officers and K9 proceeded on foot, working their way along a dense row of pine trees, the trunks of which were perfectly aligned, meaning they must have originally been planted to serve as a windbreak.

Peering through the trees, Madge spotted Tiff's car parked nearby.

"No sign of the Tacoma," she frowned.

"Maybe in the garage," Drake suggested.

"Likely," the lieutenant agreed. "Let's get closer."

When they were in range of the manor's broad front entrance, Madge picked up a handful of pebbles and hurled them at the wide wooden door. Spawning a strident racket, the pebbles bounced off the wood and clattered onto the porch. To make certain, the lieutenant repeated the process. A long interval of silence followed with no response from the manor.

"You and Mitzie take the front door," Madge whispered.

"Roger that," said Drake.

With the front door secured, Madge sidled toward the rear. Pausing midway between the front entrance and a bay window, Madge pressed her back against the exterior brick wall and unholstered her pistol. Turning toward the window, she was surprised to see her reflection.

"Mirror tint," Madge whispered those words aloud. "Figures. Got something to conceal? When in doubt, tint all your windows. Anyhow, I've gotta find a way in."

Searching for the most expedient entryway, Madge explored the manor's exterior until she reached what appeared to be a servant's entrance. This ordinary wooden door with its small eye-level window seemed to be the lone chink in an otherwise impenetrable fortress.

Madge had a warrant to search the premises, but time was of the essence and that piece of paper wasn't going to open a locked door. Father Thomas might be inside and in danger. She'd have to exercise initiative. Her current colleague, Ranger Dallas Heckleson, had a colorful opinion about breaking and entering.

"A cop who kin't open a locked door is like a hole without a donut," Heckleson was fond of saying.

Remembering that non sequitur—one of many uttered by the old ranger—always made Madge smile. She was grinning as she opened her leather pick case and manipulated the lock. She grinned even broader when a telltale click told her the lock was breached and she continued grinning as she pushed the door open. Even when she slipped inside and shouted *Police!* she was still grinning—until she wasn't.

She had passed through a kitchen and pushed into the next room when she saw it. A tall, silver-plated trophy cup stood on a fireplace mantel and draped over one handle, its conspicuous tassel drooping sideways, was Herbert Schulz's colorful and blood-stained woolen cap.

"One case solved," Madge said as she activated her radio.

Chapter 37

Post Office
(January 1 / Afternoon)

The pint-sized post office which served the Village of Lavender was closed but the hallway adjacent to the boxes was open and brightly illuminated. So, Annie Sands waited inside, hoping no one would arrive to check their mail and ask why the detective was wearing a holstered pistol in the middle of their quiet little community on this crisp winter's afternoon. Sergeant Harold Drake had dropped her off, then headed to Brimstone Road, in case their suspect occupied his place in Coal-Slide Canyon. The idea was for Drake to rendezvous with Lieutenant Madge Oxford.

"A rendezvous," Annie said aloud. "I don't suppose those two would ever—" she wondered.

An old pickup drove by and spotted the detective through the glass door. Annie managed a half-hearted wave as Marcus

Fairchild honked his horn. Then Scott Malm rolled by, driving the village's little snowplow. Another wave, another honk.

Grand Central Station, she thought to herself.

She should have worn a longer jacket to obscure the weapon, but how was she to know that she'd end up armed in such a public place? The afternoon was clear and chilly and, after fifteen minutes waiting, she decided to modify Trinidad's original plan. She was supposed to wait for her husband but, leaving the post office as she typed, Annie composed a text informing Trinidad that she was going to walk and asking him to meet her there. She hit "send" wondering how long her unreliable cellphone would take to transmit her text message.

She'd have to travel four blocks through the snowy and now mostly empty streets of Lavender to reach the old Schulz place on G Street, but anything was better than standing around. The old two-story house sat alone on the village outskirts, a lonesome structure on an undeveloped block where even the sidewalks had yet to reach. The abandoned house might have proven a tempting target for vandals. But local kids thought the place was haunted, and Annie had to agree it looked spooky enough to house a ghost or two. Thoughts of ghosts reminded her of the cryptic initials handwritten in Herb Schulz's unpublished manuscript.

She repeated the letters to herself as she walked, *C.B.G.— leaving aside the first two letters, could the 'G' refer to G Street?*

Trinidad seems to think so. Which must be why he and I are staking out the old house.

Annie was half a block away from the isolated, boarded-up house and walking along the unplowed road, when she came abreast of a line of poplars and spotted the gray Toyota parked in the driveway. Suddenly the significance of the tire tracks she'd been following in the deep snow dawned on her as she stepped aside and knelt down to examine the tread-marks. Drake had speculated that tire tracks near the Liberstein barn were made by Tacoma tires and these tracks looked similar.

Feeling suddenly exposed, Annie stood quickly up, veered off the road, and rushed through the ankle-deep snow toward the poplars. Stopping when she reached the trees which formed a single-file windbreak alongside the house, she peered between the close-knit trunks. She could see the Toyota clearly and had a full view of the side of the house. The doors and windows within her vision were still boarded up. No access there, she decided.

So, where's the driver? she asked herself, and no sooner had she entertained that thought than she spotted the answer.

At the base of the house where the outside wall met the snow, a wooden door was propped open. The door was up on its edge, at a ninety-degree angle, and she had to move her head slightly to see it properly. Like other vintage structures in Lavender, the old Schulz house would have a coal cellar and this door would be that cellar's outside entrance.

Coal bin—G Street, she told herself as her racing mind deciphered Schulz's handwritten note.

To confirm her observations, Annie looked again at the outside wall and saw the outline of another opening—a recessed square of hinged metal marking the upper end of the household's coal repository. A century or more ago, a coal wagon would have been parked in the space occupied by the Toyota while workers inserted a chute into the house's coal door and sent a stream of so-called black diamonds cascading into the basement. Annie could almost imagine the racket as lumps of coal clattered their way down the metal chute. But in reality, she could hear nothing except the sound of winter wind vibrating through the up-turned slats of the wooden basement door.

Just at that moment, her cellphone pinged. It was a message from Trinidad.

"Stay put, don't—" she started to read, but her attention was drawn away as a shot rang out from the direction of the house. Seconds later, she spotted Father Thomas scrambling awkwardly out of the basement. He fell face-first into the snow and scuttled under the Toyota, flailing his arms and legs like a swimmer doing a dog paddle on land. Despite the desperation of the scene, Annie couldn't help being amazed at how agile the old pastor had suddenly become.

Without a clear idea of what she was doing but, determined to provide cover for the cowering and possibly wounded man, Annie pulled her pistol, abandoned the poplars, and ran in a crouch toward the Toyota.

Sliding to a stop beside the vehicle, she bent down and whispered to Father Thomas.

"I'm here," she said.

"What?" said Thomas. The old man turned his head toward Annie and seemed dazed.

"Are you hurt?" she asked.

"No—no," Thomas repeated. "But God help me, I think I've killed someone. I wrestled the pistol away and it discharged and—"

"Father!" A voice sounded from the deep recesses of the basement. "You old weasel! You had better run because when I come up these stairs, I will put a bullet in your—" the voice seemed to falter. "Right in the middle of your bald, lying forehead!"

"Stay here," Annie commanded Father Thomas even though she was certain the disoriented clergyman had no intention of moving.

Skirting past the Toyota, Annie moved rapidly along the side of the house. She stopped behind the up-turned cellar door with her back pressed against the outer wall and the door's rusted hinges at her feet. There were narrow chinks between the slats of weathered wood, but she was fairly certain she was well-hidden behind the vertical door. An oversized restraining hook had been securely screwed into the wall beside her. The hook itself had been inserted into a round eyelet on the door, forming a firm connection which held the door in place.

Peering through the slats in case the shooter should emerge from the coal cellar, she holstered her pistol. Then she used both hands to carefully disengage the hook while simultaneously lacing her fingers into the eyelet so that her tight grip held the teetering door in place. Standing there, striving to keep her balance in the snow, she felt the heavy door tugging to be free. If the owner of that threatening voice came up the cellar stairs, she'd let go and flatten the unlucky villain—whoever he was.

Annie was tensed to act until she recognized the hum of the Ridgeline's engine and glanced over her shoulder to see Trinidad's vehicle sliding into the driveway. Momentarily distracted by the unfamiliar flashing lights on the dashboard of her husband's familiar Honda, she took her eyes off the cellar door. Even before the Honda came to a stop, Trinidad jumped out and the Ridgeline bumped softly into the Toyota as he rushed in her direction with his pistol drawn.

Looking back toward the cellar door, Annie saw the barrel of a machine pistol emerging into the cold winter air. It was a fleeting glimpse, but she acted on instinct and, just as the weapon fired, she released her grip. The freed door slammed instantly downward, simultaneously dislodging the pistol and knocking the shooter back down the cellar stairs while the careening weapon sprayed a volley of errant shots in the direction of the poplars.

"Holy cats!" Trinidad exclaimed as he reached his bride's side and tackled her to the ground.

"And hello to you too," Annie said, and she managed a nervous laugh as the two detectives lay sprawled together in the snow, entwined like earnest lovers, with a layer of icy flakes taking the place of satin sheets. Lying next to his bride, Trinidad glanced across the driveway and spotted the prostrate form of Father Thomas still cowering beneath the Toyota.

"Father?" he asked.

"Detective," Thomas said in greeting.

"Stay put," Trinidad suggested.

"You bet," said Thomas.

All three remained on the ground, listening to the welcome sound of sirens streaming to the rescue. The approaching cacophony seemed to be coming from every direction until the decibels converged and no fewer than seven patrol cars crowded over the frozen lawn and driveway of the abandoned Schulz house. A platoon of officers emerged from the congregating vehicles and, after ushering the civilians out of the way, Madge and Sergeant Drake cautiously pulled the cellar door open.

At the bottom of the concrete stairs, they discovered the unconscious, crumpled form of Karl Bistro with a sizeable knot on his head, a bandaged arm, and a minor bullet wound in one leg. An ambulance arrived, the paramedics looking a bit frazzled as they strapped the injured man to a gurney and hoisted the immobilized prisoner out of the basement.

"You guys going for the record?" asked Andrew as he balanced one end of the gurney.

"I got the same question," said Bobby as he and his partner lugged the stretcher toward their waiting ambulance. "Between our favorite lieutenant at the church and then the Surface Creek crew across town at what's her name's farm and now this neighborhood cluster-crap, that's three calls in two hours. And we ain't even had time for a sandwich. Maybe we should go for a ballot initiative to get more help."

"Good luck with that," said Madge. "Wait! Hold on!" the lieutenant requested.

Before Andrew closed the ambulance hatch, Madge signaled for Drake to climb in to provide security, telling the sergeant that someone would drive his patrol car back.

"Can Mitzie come too?" Drake asked.

"Care if our K9 rides along?" Madge asked the paramedic.

"Help yourself," said Bobby as he slid to one side to make room for the officer and the dog. "From what the radio chatter says, we've already got a weasel on board, so what's one more critter more or less?"

Everyone shared a good laugh until another radio call burst their balloon. The sad news reached the paramedics and every one of the sheriff's crew at the same time.

"*10-0-0* officer down at the Lavender car wash," said the dispatcher. "Bad news—somebody really needs to get over there. Over."

Chapter 38

A Barrel of Nickels
(January 21, 2020)

Three weeks later, the principal actors from the Delta County investigation were sitting around a crowded conference table in the station's cramped meeting room. The mood was somber in the days following Dallas Heckleson's funeral—a melancholy indulgence which the old ranger, if he had lived, would probably have roundly discouraged. As it was, the conference room was packed with a mixture of badges and civilians.

"We need another one," Sheriff Jack Treadway pleaded as Lieutenant Madge Oxford returned empty-handed from her quest to secure more chairs.

"That's all we got," said Madge. "Unless you want Sharon taking calls standing up."

"I don't need a place to sit," said Sergeant Harold Drake as he stood up and invited the lieutenant to take his chair.

"A gentleman at last," Madge said, and Annie noticed that her cheeks flushed as she and Drake exchanged a glance while she took a seat.

"Everybody comfortable?" asked Jack who'd also noticed the fleeting look which had passed between Sergeant Drake and Delta County's capable lieutenant. He noted also that the now-standing Drake remained conspicuously close to Madge with his hand resting on the back of her chair. Even his K9 had assumed a protective stance next to Madge's chair. The symptoms of budding affection seemed palpable. Jack cleared his throat as he opened the three-ring notebook which lay on the table before him.

"Has anybody not read my preliminary criminal case report?" Jack asked.

As if in response, Mitzie let out an unrehearsed bark which caused the room to erupt in laughter.

"Aside from our resourceful police dog, has everybody else already read this?" Jack looked around the table at his officers who nodded in turn. Then he got eye-contact with the Village of Lavender's resourceful detectives who also nodded and rewarded him with a pair of approving smiles.

It's good, the expressions of Annie and Trinidad Sands seemed to say, *to see our favorite sheriff acting like his old self again.*

Jack smiled back and then turned serious as his gaze fell on the five reporters—one each from TV and radio; an online blogger; and two print journalists—all of whom also nodded. Lastly, he looked at Jim Dean who nodded as well.

"Good," the sheriff said. "So, let's see if we can sort out what the hell just happened a few short weeks ago durin' our ordinarily uneventful extended holiday break. So, ladies and gents, in a moment I'll direct your attention to the whiteboard where our resident artist, Detective Mrs. Annie Sands, has sketched a helpful diagram."

Scattered applause and another bark followed this tribute.

"But first, a moment of silence in honor of our fallen comrade, Dallas Heckleson, Texas Ranger Emeritus, stalwart friend and fellow officer."

A reverent hush fell over the room and even the eager-beaver media types paused in silent reflection.

"Amen," said Jack. "Now, please note for the record—" at this point Jack glanced overhead toward the microphone which dangled from the ceiling and then looked directly into the red light on the camera which the county videographer was manning in the rear of the room. "Please note that Tiffany Northbridge, Delta County medical examiner, is absent—" Jack lingered a moment and seemed to falter before he continued. "Absent and recovering from injuries, but she is represented by Jim Dean, interim examiner, who I presume has studied Miss Northbridge's notes."

"Indeed," said Jim.

"So, chime-in as needed," said the sheriff.

"Indeed, I shall," said Jim. "And may I say—?" but a stern look from Jack caused the new man to cut his statement short.

And the honeymoon is over, thought the officious Mr. Dean.

"Annie," said Jack, "the floor is yours."

Trinidad was beaming at his bride as she stood and walked to the whiteboard.

"The war nickel," Annie began as her voice modulated into a self-assured and professorial tone. "None of us in this room was alive to remember World War II, let alone appreciate the irrational Nazi plot which, more than seven decades ago, had been hastily conceived in a vain attempt to erode the Allied cause. And yet, here in Western Colorado, we were surrounded by elders who not only recalled the war but were also instrumental in salvaging souvenirs of Adolph Hitler's shrewd and diabolical war nickel scheme."

Annie paused to study her audience and smiled to see that she had their undivided attention. In particular, the reporters were hanging on her every word and no wonder. Only Jack and she and Trinidad knew the full details of this convoluted story—insights which the three of them had gleaned from their exposure to Herbert Schulz's unpublished manuscript. Others knew pieces of the tale and may have guessed the rest, but some were hearing all this for the first time.

"Go on, honey," prompted Madge in an exaggerated stage whisper.

Annie blushed, then reached into her shirt pocket and pulled out her prop.

"The war nickel," she said as she held the unassuming coin aloft like a magician revealing an unexpected white rabbit. "One of several thousand found hidden under layers of coal in a basement bin beneath the former home of Lavender's dearest residents, Mr. and Mrs. Herbert and Meeska Schulz. The lab techs are still sifting through the coal, but so far, they've extracted enough five-cent pieces to fill every inch of a 53-gallon hogshead barrel. And this cache represents only one of an estimated hundred-thousand barrels produced by the Nazis in 1942. Why so many nickels?"

Annie paused as Jim Dean raised his hand either innocently or on purpose in an effort to spoil the impact of what she'd intended as a rhetorical question.

"I'll tell you why," she continued as she noticed Jack walking over to pop Dean on the back of the head and whisper something in the ear of the overly-eager clinician. Annie grinned broadly before continuing her recitation. "The Nazis had a plan to use their network of clandestine North American agents to introduce millions of counterfeit Jefferson-head nickels into the 1942 American economy. However wrong-headed their plan may seem to modern observers, their intention was to incite a financial panic, thereby undermining faith in democracy during a fragile summer when the war was not going so well for us. Remember that in the 1940s a true nickel was widely used to activate American vending machines and pay telephones and as a token to pay for transport on buses and trains—not to mention their essential role in gaining access to auto-mat food vending machines and the occasional pay-toilet.

"In America, nickels were minted with strict weight specifications in order to serve each coin's multiple purposes. Even when the metals used to create nickels were required to support the American war effort and a new combination of less-vital metals was used to mint legitimate war nickels, those newly-minted coins were meticulously designed and correctly-weighted.

"Beginning sometime after 1941 and America's entry into the war, the enemy hatched a scheme to manufacture thousands upon thousands of counterfeit war nickels. Minted by slave labor in the outskirts of Berlin, these bogus nickels were composed of an alloy which was, by intentional design, too light to trip coin-operated mechanisms. And the Nazis reasoned that injecting a flood of plug nickels into the U.S. economy would gum up everyday life and engender chaos."

"So, then, why didn't they do it?" interrupted one of the journalists.

"That's a great question," said Annie, not skipping a beat. "And, for the answer to that and many other questions, we turned to a fantastic source—something Karl Bistro tried but failed to obtain. Namely, the entirety of Herbert Schulz's unpublished manuscript which not only describes the war nickel scheme, but also chronicles how three local residents are connected to it."

Annie paused for effect.

"Herb's manuscript reveals why the 1942 plot was, literally, scrapped," she said. "It was abandoned for the simple reason that somebody in the Third Reich—Herbert suggests it was some guy with a mop of hair and a funny moustache. Anyway, somebody changed their mind, and the nickel scheme was abandoned in favor of counterfeiting the British pound note instead. Raw materials were growing scarce in Germany, and somebody decided to stop using scarce metallic resources to mint the war nickels. In the end, literally overnight, most of the bogus nickels were rapidly melted down to support the German war effort—all but a single barrelful which became part of the dowry of a teenaged orphan and war bride who, barrel and all, crossed the Atlantic in 1946 to become the new wife of Herbert Schulz."

"Meeska," said the blogger.

"Meeska," Annie confirmed as she concluded her history lesson and directed her audience's attention to the whiteboard on which she had written the name of the German bride with Herbert Schulz beside it. The couple's names were embedded in a heart and united by a plus sign. The Schulz's names appeared at the top of the board with a single arrow pointing down to Annie's well-rendered sketch of a wooden barrel. Below the barrel were two more arrows, each arrowhead pointing toward the container with the shafts radiating outward to intersect with two additional names: *Wolfgang Kjolhede (aka, Father Thomas) and Gerda Vogel (aka, Caroline Liberstein.)*

Annie explained that two Delta County residents had been prisoners during the war. Thomas had been a Danish freedom fighter captured in Holland. Caroline was a Jewish newlywed who had been swept up in Poland by the conquering Nazis. Thomas, Caroline, and her late husband Otto had all been transported to a German concentration camp and then to a foundry on the Ruhr River where, among other wartime projects, they helped mint the war nickels.

Otto Vogel died in the work camp—the victim of insidious medical experiments. Caroline was heartbroken by the death of her husband and doubly traumatized when she too was forced to endure sinister medical procedures. Thomas was also subjected to medical experimentation. They both emerged from the Nazi clinics with a bitter desire to do all they could to frustrate their captors. Later, when she and Thomas were ordered to destroy the nickels, they conspired with a local baker to smuggle a single barrel out of the factory. As fate would have it, the conspiring baker turned out to be Meeska's uncle. The agreement had been to hide the barrel until after the war when the coins might be of some value in a conflict-ravaged land where all other currency would have ceased to have meaning.

Like so many in Europe of that generation, the conspirators became separated after the war and only reunited years later, whereupon the uncle divulged that he had sent the barrel to America along with his only living niece. Having changed their names to Thomas and Caroline, the two ex-slaves and unwilling medical subjects, made their way to the States and instantly settled in Western Colorado. Their plan was to keep an eye on Meeska and her new husband, all the while biding their time and hoping to recover a treasure which they felt was rightfully theirs.

But the refugees soon found that their shared experience of surviving the war formed a stronger bond than some vague and less honorable notion of somehow profiting from the nickels. So, the two old comrades and Meeska and Herbert soon became a fast foursome. Little did the friends suspect that the youngest and healthiest among them—darling Meeska—would be the first to die. At her wake, the three survivors—Thomas (who'd found God), Caroline (who'd discovered potato farming), and Herbert (who mourned his dear wife)—made a pact. They would bury both Meeska and the nickels and never speak of the latter again.

Annie was about to continue when one of the reporters interrupted.

"Tell us again how you happen to know all this."

"As I said, our informed source was Herbert Schulz' unpublished manuscript," Annie explained. "Herbert, with Meeska's help, co-authored a memoire in which they documented facts and named names."

"Is this document—" asked the blogger, but Jack had anticipated her question.

"The Schulz manuscript is even now with a Western Colorado printer, and it'll hit bookstores by next Christmas with proceeds donated to support local and statewide veteran's organizations," Jack said and when the hue and cry of the media folks died down, the sheriff added. "Naturally you'll all be provided, as soon as practical, with advance copies. Now, Mrs. Sands, please continue."

"Into this idyllic agreement," Annie continued, "a sinister entity recently inserted their murderous agent, one Corporal Karl Bistro, S.B."

"S.B. for—?" one of the reporters prompted.

"The initials stand for our old infamous adversaries, the Scarlet Brotherhood," Annie answered. "A shadowy Russian mob which, I'm sorry to say, keeps popping up here in Western Colorado."

"Like a bad penny," Trinidad agreed.

"Or, in this case," Jack quipped, "like a bad nickel. It appears that either the Russian mob or a renegade cell of Neo-Nazis—we're still tryin' to sort out which—had employed Bistro to track down local folks associated with the bogus war nickels."

"But what was this Bistro character's end game?" the reporter asked. "We understand from your talk and your media kit that the original batch of millions of counterfeit nickels was supposed to be smuggled into America. And we get that each bogus war nickel was intended to gum up the works of wartime vending machines and so on. To sow mistrust and dissension—to create some kind of nationwide panic. But you say the scheme was dropped when the Nazis needed the metal to support the war effort. So, to make more weapons, all the coins were confiscated and melted down."

"All but one barrel," Jack clarified.

"Yes," the reporter continued, his tone impatient. "We understand all that. But what makes the contents of that single barrel so important—so valuable? It's not as if America still runs on vending machines and pay telephones—even nickel slot machines, which once held sway in casinos, are out of favor these days. Was Bistro's organization planning to dump the coins into the marketplace to deflate the value of legitimate and collectable war nickels? That seems like small potatoes to me. Or did they maybe plan to melt the nickels down in order to extract and sell the metal? Why did this barrel of German coins end up on the murderous and greedy radar of some very bad hombres? And what makes these nickels something worth killing for?"

"I presume that most of us here are aware of the class of elements known as *rare earth minerals*," Annie said.

"Yeah," said the blogger whose youthful appearance suggested she was a member of the Gen Z cohort. "Rare earths are elements from one of the bottom rungs of the Periodic Table which are vital to the electronics industry, the production of powerful magnets, and the future of perpetual battery power. There are rare earth components in our cellphones, our computers, our cars, and our televisions. And governments around the globe are aggressively competing to locate rare earths and yank them out of the ground."

"Couldn't have said it better," Annie agreed. "In the 1940s, the Nazi chemists didn't know exactly what they had when they adopted the rare earth element *Lanthanum* as the main alloy used to further their bogus nickel scheme." She paused to spell out the unfamiliar term for the reporters. "They merely recognized that the stuff mixed well with other metals. They also saw that it was bright and silvery in appearance and so soft that it could be shaped with a butterknife before being annealed into rounded discs and stamped into bogus coins. Fast-forward to now and this particular rare earth mineral is, literally, worth its weight in gold—probably more. These days scientists are continually discovering new uses for its unique properties and researchers are also revisiting the potential that small and systematically administered dosages of Lanthanum may yield medicinal benefits."

"Medicinal benefits?" the blogger noted. "So does that explain this *immortal Nazi* idea that we keep hearing rumors about?"

"Yes, how about this immortal business?" demanded several other voices.

"I—" Jack began.

"If I may," a voice sounded from shadows in the rear of the room, then the words were repeated. "If I may—"

"As you were!" A booming, and obviously military, voice echoed in the crowded room as a broad-shouldered sergeant in fatigues demanded attention. For a full minute in the wake of this unambiguous command, the crowded conference room was enveloped in an expectant silence.

"Allow me to introduce Colonel Malcolm West," said Jack. "Colonel West, the floor is yours."

"Thank you," said the colonel as he made his way to the front of the room and stood before the group. The colonel was a tall and imposing man who wore the full military dress uniform of an Air Force officer. "Ladies and gentlemen, I have been authorized to read into the official record of these proceedings a statement by the President, who is this day conducting the Nation's business in Switzerland at the Davos World Economic Forum. I quote:

"To the residents of Western Colorado, greetings. Local and regional law enforcement officers are to be commended for their role in bringing to justice the international war criminal known as Corporal Karl Bistro. Corporal Bistro has been extradited to be tried in a future action to be administered by the International Court of Justice under the auspices of the United Nations. Judicial proceedings are delayed at present while Corporal Bistro's mental fitness is evaluated. The prisoner's claims to have lived for an unnaturally lengthy period of time without any signs of appreciable aging have been unanimously and vigorously dismissed as a fabrication of neo-Nazi propaganda.

The United States of America will issue no further comment on this closed subject. Respectfully submitted—"

The remainder of the statement's closing valediction was drowned out by the ensuing commotion as the room erupted in a frenzy of shouted questions, appeals for more information, and general tumult.

Epilogue

Leaving aside the fanciful and also chilling notion of an immortal Nazi, the case of The War Nickel Murders remains a sobering one for Detectives Annie and Trinidad Sands. Not only did the case's principal villain take the lives of their dear friends Dallas Heckleson and Herbert Schulz, but Karl Bistro's heinous crimes also disrupted the idyllic atmosphere of the Village of Lavender.

The evils perpetrated by Bistro and his unknown masters indelibly tainted the psyche of Western Colorado. To prevent further desecration, the bodies of Herbert and Meeska Schulz were relocated and laid to rest in an undisclosed location. Tiff Northbridge walked away from forensic work, took a vow of poverty, moved to Nicaragua, and spent her time volunteering to build schools and improve village water systems. Father Thomas retired from his church and returned to flourish in his native Denmark. The Schulz house in Lavender was demolished to make way for a new affordable housing development. Two months after entrenching herself in Herbert Schulz's isolated cabin, Caroline Liberstein went for an early morning hike and vanished somewhere in the wilds of the Grand Mesa.

Two huge explosions rocked the Village. A bomb disposal team from Tooele Army Depot in Utah arrived to supervise the search of Karl Bistro's garage. The soldiers had managed to crack the code of that fortress-like structure and had dispatched a robot to detect and diffuse explosive ordnance when a series of blasts leveled the place, erasing any chance to gather further evidence. The late Ranger Heckleson's isolated house in the 'dobies was purchased by foreign investors who, out of ignorance or by design, allowed renters to establish a methamphetamine laboratory on the premises. An enormous eruption ended this clandestine enterprise and pulverized the Heckleson homestead.

In April 2020, the region survived a series of computer glitches which may or may not be attributed to Bistro and his cohorts. Sheriff Jack Treadway had to consult a cybercrime investigator to track down and disable an impish artificial intelligence robot—which in the jargon of computer geeks can be reduced to the term AI bot. For weeks this technological gremlin wreaked havoc on local internet services. The rogue AI bot added an extra five cents to every Delta County water bill until it switched gears to infiltrate community calendars in order to arbitrarily cancel and reschedule local concerts, book club meetings, high school sporting events, and writing group seminars. For a time, county computers were maliciously encrypted, cutting off employee access and essentially holding organizational data hostage until malware was discovered and removed from the system. During these hectic weeks, everyone braced for a monetary ransom demand which, thankfully, did not materialize.

Meanwhile, the cache of counterfeit war nickels was sent by rail to the Denver Mint, but the coins vanished in transit. Herbert Schulz's manuscript was never published in book form. All copies of the draft were confiscated by agents of Homeland Security, and during the chaos of the global Covid-19 pandemic, those impounded copies were mislaid.

Karl Bistro escaped from the custody of international police, and he remains at large. His exact whereabouts and activities are unknown.

Acknowledgments

I wish to acknowledge the invaluable work of my earnest Beta readers. Four brave souls took time to read and comment on the first drafts of this novel. Their vital input helped shape and refine my story. Heartfelt thanks go out to Mary Bruno, Don Burch, Stacy Malmgren, and Kim Taylor.

Much love to my dear wife, Donna Marie, who keeps me fed, keeps the coffee coming, and gently admonishes me when, after writing for hours, it is time to come to bed. She continues to be my inspiration and the light of my life.

Equal affection to my brother Tom, sister-in-law Sharon, and Leonard, my dearly-departed father, all of whom continually remind me of the gift of family.

I am much indebted to readers who have faithfully followed my main characters, Trinidad and Annie Sands, through three previous books in this set of mysteries. Their loyalty, insightful reviews, and supporting purchases have sustained me in my work.

Those who follow my writing know that my main female character is based on a combination of my late friend Tina Kjolhede; my sainted mother, Carol Ruth (Quick) Benjamin; and my sister Ann. Stillborn as an infant in October 1942, Ann lived only a few hours. She never experienced life and so I've dedicated my writing to giving her memory an opportunity to blossom.

Donald Paul Benjamin
July 2024

About the Author

Donald Paul Benjamin is an American novelist who specializes in cozy mysteries and high fantasy. His writing includes elements of romance and humor. He also writes about Western Colorado history. He is the author of *The Four Corners Mystery Series, The Great Land Fantasy Series and The Surface Creek Life Series.*

In addition to his writing career, he also works as a freelance journalist, cartoonist, and photographer. A U.S. Army veteran, he served three years as a military journalist and illustrator, including a tour in Korea. Trained as a teacher of reading, he has worked with a wide variety of learners from those attending kindergarten to college students. He also holds an advanced degree in college administration. He lived in Arizona and worked in higher education for more than three decades before retiring in 2014.

He now lives in Cedaredge, a small town on the Western Slope of Colorado, where he hikes and fishes in the surrounding wilderness. He and his wife, Donna Marie, operate **Elevation Press of Colorado**, a service which helps independent authors self-publish their works (see information on the following page).

Email: elevationpressbooks@gmail.com
Studio Phone: 970-856-9891
Mail: D.P. Benjamin, P.O. Box 603, Cedaredge, CO 81413
Website: https://benjaminauthor.com/
Visit the Author's Facebook Page under: D.P. Benjamin Author
Instagram: https://www.instagram.com/benjaminnovelist/

The Four Corners Mystery Series
- **Book 1:** *The Road to Lavender*
- **Book 2:** *A Lavender Wedding*
- **Book 3:** *Spirits of Grand Lake*
- **Book 4:** *The War Nickel Murders*
- **Book 5:** *Rare Earth*
- **Book 6:** *Walking Horse Ranch*
- **Book 7:** *Lavender Farewell*

The Great Land Fantasy Series
- **Book 1:** *Stone Bride*
- **Book 2:** *Iron Angel*
- **Book 3:** *Redhackle*
- **Book 4:** *Bindbuilder*
- **Book 5:** *Nachtfalke*
- **Book 6:** *Isochronuous*
- **Book 7:** *Ruth and Esau*

The Surface Creek Life Series
- **Book 1:** *A Surface Creek Christmas: Winter Tales 1904–1910*

In paperback or Kindle on **amazon.com** and **barnesandnoble.com**.

Previews of Future Publications

Mountain: A Cautionary Tale

In the autumn of 2024, the author will publish a novel containing all episodes of the serialized story which has appeared weekly in the *High Country Spotlight/Shopper*. **Mountain: A Cautionary Tale** is an alternative history covering 1936-1941. Set along the Kansas-Colorado border, it's the story of a misguided man, his star-crossed family, and an enormous public works project gone terribly wrong.

A Lavender Trilogy

In 2025, the author will celebrate his 80th birthday. In recognition of this milestone, the final three books in The Four Corners Mystery Series will be written as three novellas. This trilogy of short novels will be melded into a single published book. Three distinct adventures titled **Rare Earth, Walking Horse Ranch,** and **Lavender Farewell** will chronicle and conclude the adventures of Detectives Trinidad and Annie Sands.

ELEVATION PRESS
OF COLORADO

Your One-Stop Publishing Option

Established 1976

As an independent publisher, we are actively seeking authors who desire to publish their work. For such individuals, we provide design and formatting services. Starting with an author's Microsoft Word document, we produce a book cover and interior pages which the author can submit to a traditional printer or to a print-on-demand service, such as Kindle Direct Publishing (KDP) or IngramSpark. Depending on the complexity of your book, we may also be able to convert the print PDF into a reflowable e-book.

We have successfully formatted a variety of published books including memoirs, children's books, novels, and works of non-fiction.

For more information, visit our website:

elevation-press-books.com

Made in the USA
Columbia, SC
27 December 2024